**GLEN WU (AKA GLUE,** ...

He's returned to Hong Kong, the city he grew up in, and he's teaching ESL, just to placate his parents. But he shows up hungover to class, barely stays awake, and prefers to spend his time smoking up until dawn breaks.

As he watches the city he loves fall—the protests, the brutal arrests—life continues around him. So he drinks more, picks more fights with his drug dealer friend, thinks loftier thoughts about the post-colonial condition and Frantz Fanon. The very little he does care about: his sister, who deals with Hong Kong's demise by getting engaged to a rich immigration consultant; his on-and-off-again relationship with a woman who steals things from him; and memories of someone he once met in Canada . . .

When the government tightens its grip, language starts to lose all meaning for Glue, and he finds himself pulled into an unsettling venture, ultimately culminating in an act of violence.

Inventive and utterly irresistible, with QR codes woven throughout, Sheung-King's ingenious novel encapsulates the anxieties and apathies of the millennial experience. *Batshit Seven* is an ode to a beloved city, an indictment of the cycles of imperialism, and a reminder of the beautiful things left under the hype of commodified living.

"Sheung-King has crafted a novel of dazzling scope: global and deeply personal, all at once. It's uncompromisingly honest, smart, and hilarious—in the best, saddest way."
—KAI THOMAS, AUTHOR OF *IN THE UPPER COUNTRY*

"Sheung-King's erudite riffs on language, meaning, and the constantly dislocating experiences of modern existence make *Batshit Seven* surprising, bizarre, and perhaps most of all, fun."
—NABEN RUTHNUM, AUTHOR OF *A HERO OF OUR TIME*

"Like a glass-bottom boat tour of the millennial mind."
—MICHAEL LAPOINTE, AUTHOR OF *THE CREEP*

"Playful, energetic, and propelled by hypnotic prose, *Batshit Seven* is a cunning dissection of our corporate age. Elegantly styled and full of raucous humour, Sheung-King has wrought a precise, glimmering gem that twists and turns in the mind long after it's read."
—ADNAN KHAN, AUTHOR OF *THERE HAS TO BE A KNIFE*

"A wild and twisted symphony of concise, staccato writing and crescendoing narrative. . . . I was transfixed from the opening note to the closing word. This novel truly shows how different literary worlds can crash together in devastatingly cool ways. Another masterpiece of fiction from one of the freshest voices in Asian Canadian lit today."
—JENNY HEIJUN WILLS, AUTHOR OF *OLDER SISTER. NOT NECESSARILY RELATED.*

# BATSHIT SEVEN

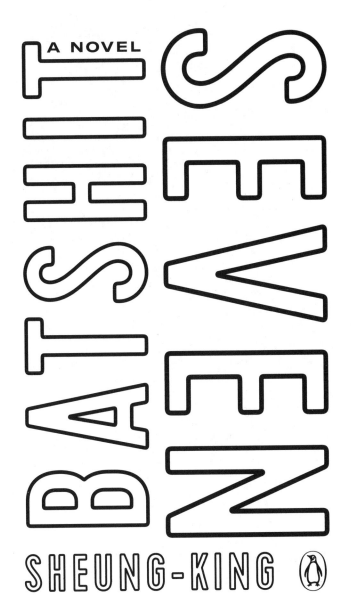

A NOVEL

BATSHIT SEVEN

SHEUNG-KING

PENGUIN

an imprint of Penguin Canada, a division of Penguin Random House Canada Limited

Canada • USA • UK • Ireland • Australia •
New Zealand • India • South Africa • China

First published 2024

www.penguinrandomhouse.ca

Portions of this book have previously appeared, in different form, in the following: *The Capilano Review; The Spirits Have Nothing to Do with Us: New Chinese Canadian Fiction*, edited by Dan K. Woo; *filling Station; Fatal Flaw*; and on blue-metropolis.org, uoguelph.ca, and singaporeunbound.org.

*Publisher's note: This book is a work of fiction. Names, characters, places and incidents either are the product of the author's imagination or are used fictitiously, and any resemblance to actual persons living or dead, events, or locales is entirely coincidental.*

As of the time of initial publication, the QR codes displayed in this book link to existing websites on the Internet. Penguin Random House Canada is not responsible for, and should not be deemed to endorse or recommend, any website other than its own or any content available on the Internet (including without limitation at any website, blog page, information page) that is not created by Penguin Random House Canada.

LIBRARY AND ARCHIVES CANADA CATALOGUING IN PUBLICATION

Title: Batshit seven / Sheung-King.
Names: Sheung-King, 1994- author.
Identifiers: Canadiana (print) 20220424284 | Canadiana (ebook) 20220424314 |
    ISBN 9780735245303 (hardcover) | ISBN 9780735245310 (EPUB)
Classification: LCC PS8637.H48955 B38 2023 | DDC C813/.6—dc23

Book design by Matthew Flute
Cover design by Matthew Flute
Cover image: (background) © oxygen / Moment / Getty Images

Printed in the United States of America

10 9 8 7 6 5 4 3 2 1

Penguin
Random House
PENGUIN CANADA

For Prisca

# BATSHIT SEVEN

# WE

# ARE

# IMAGINED

# BODIES

**SHATTERED GLASS** is vibrating noiselessly inside Glue's head. He is hungover. The air-conditioned room dried all his sweat from last night, leaving a layer of sandy grease atop his skin. Glue looks up at the ceiling. It is perfectly white. Glue tries not to blink, stares so hard that he becomes lost in this ocean of whiteness. Yet when he shuts his eyes, the broken glass inside of his head reverberates, making him nauseated. The noiseless shaking of glass, an emblem of entropy, forms in his mind, a dark sea consisting of a thousand waves and no earth.

Now that Glue has been back in Hong Kong for six months, he is beginning to realize that nothing ever changes. Everything that seems to change is a repetition of something that has already happened. Glue lived with his sister, Gwen, when he was eighteen. The two shared a two-bedroom apartment in Toronto. And before the two moved to Canada for undergrad, Gwen and Glue lived with their parents, in the same apartment that Glue is living in now. Situated at the end of the orange subway line, this apartment in Tung Chung, an area located on Lantau Island, is a thirty-minute subway ride from the city's centre, at the edge of Hong Kong, near the airport. Eight apartment buildings, four on either side, form Tung Chung Crescent above the Tung Chung MTR station. In the middle of the crescent is an outdoor swimming pool, a basketball court, and a clubhouse with a gym, two tennis courts, a small garden, badminton courts, and indoor playgrounds for children. Glue likes this about Tung Chung: he can hear the planes taking off at night. Glue feels comforted knowing that the airport is only ten minutes away.

**"SNOW IS WHITE"** *is true if and only if snow is white.* This sentence from a class Glue dropped at university lingers in his mind when May tells him that she stole something of his.

"I need to tell you that I stole something of yours." It is four in the afternoon. They're at a bar across from the Tung Chung station, right downstairs from Glue's apartment. "I'm sorry," May says. May, like most Hong Kongers who studied abroad, chose to study in England and speaks English with a hint of a British accent.

Glue looks around. Nothing is white. The air, polluted, musty, mouth-fucks him when he breathes, leaving a taste of dust on the surface of his tongue. He could have showered before leaving his apartment, but he didn't. Glue is beginning to like the feeling of moistness.

*I need to tell you that I stole something of yours.* Need to tell him? Glue is not prepared to process this information. Instead, he thinks more about snow being white. In what class did he learn this sentence? Why did he drop that class? Glue remembers sitting in class and hearing the sentence *"Snow is white" is true if and only if snow is white*. The word "snow" reminds Glue of Hong Kong's dry winters which reminds Glue of Chinese New Year. One Chinese New Year, when they were kids, Gwen was sick and missed a large family dinner. Glue collected red pockets for Gwen. But Glue was a greedy child. He hid all the red pockets at the bottom of his underwear drawer. Gwen did not try to take the red pockets that belonged to her back from Glue. It was during the next Chinese New Year, when the two returned home with their red pockets, that Gwen told Glue that she knew he had taken the red pockets that belonged to her. This sent a chill through Glue's spine.

No one, as far as Glue knows, not even Gwen, has ever stolen anything from him. When May tells Glue that she stole something of his, the same chill rushes through him. Glue tries to speak to May but his tongue is as dry as the pieces of oven-dried seaweed he saw an influencer make on TikTok yesterday. He takes a sip of water. If he drinks too much, he will puke. Before he got into bed last night, Glue chugged a bottle of water and downed two painkillers, which usually works. Having been a heavy drinker before he dropped out of graduate school, Glue should know. But it didn't work. After consuming five beers and smoking four joints with Po-Wing last night, he feels as though there is a construction site stationed at the top of his mind, limiting his thoughts, and now May is telling him that she stole something of his. Instead of answering May, Glue considers tasting his own sweat. Does the taste of one's sweat change in accordance with one's health? Probably. Glue remembers some video on TikTok discussing the taste of sweat. Maybe he should find out. Glue, at this point, is becoming more and more aware of his body, of the stickiness between his chin and his neck.

Tasting his own sweat would probably make him puke. But maybe Glue, at this moment, wants to puke. He will back up his chair and puke all over the floor, right in front of May. It will be like an absurdist comedy sketch. Glue, the buffoon, pukes all over the floor upon hearing that something of his was stolen. What would the subtext of such a sketch be?

"What did you steal?" Glue finally manages to ask.

It is May's turn to be silent. Others on the patio continue to chat. A group of cabin attendants, bros, with loose neckties and perfectly coiffed hair, order another round of beer. May, in her pale pink Nike Dri-FIT Legend T-shirt and her hair tied tightly into a bun, does not seem to care the slightest about the airport bros.

"It's nothing important. I doubt you will even notice that anything is missing."

Glue is confused. What is the point of stealing it then? "Then why'd you have to tell me?"

"I wasn't going to. But lately I've been feeling as though a shrimp appeared inside my heart." May looks down into the darkness of her dark beer. "It's diving deeper every second, this shrimp, trying to get to the lowest point. But it doesn't know that my heart has no bottom. Inside my bottomless heart, a shrimp keeps sinking. I know the only way to get rid of this feeling is to tell you that I stole something of yours."

May, who is usually chatty and direct, does not usually sound like this.

Maybe she didn't actually steal anything of Glue's. Maybe she just needs to tell him that she did. Maybe that is why she said *I need to tell you* that I stole something of yours.

"Whatever." Glue gives up. "Why didn't you respond to any of my messages last week?"

May does not answer his question.

Glue remembers the two rules they decided on when they first started sleeping together. Don't talk politics—this is the first rule. The second rule they have is that they do not have to answer questions they do not want to.

**GLUE**, after May pays the bill and leaves, sits for a bit longer. He stares at the plate of nachos May ordered. Glue does not have the appetite to finish the nachos. He continues thinking about snow being white and whether May stole something of his. He stares at the children running around the fountain. Next to the Tung Chung MTR station is a musical fountain. On the weekends, at around seven or eight in the evening, lasers from the four corners of this large square beam pink, blue, and orange lights onto the water that ejaculates from the ground, reaching almost three storeys high, before falling and rising in accordance with the rhythms of orchestral music. Audiences are advised to watch the performance from a two-metre distance.

Neither Glue nor his sister, Gwen, played in the fountain after school; they played the piano. Gwen was quite good, Glue was terrible. His fingers weren't coordinated, and, because of his dyslexia, he could not read score. The dots that sat between the fine black lines of the white page meant nothing to him. There was no way that Glue could translate the dots into movements of his fingers, into sounds. But in spite of this, Glue and Gwen both attended a private music school in Diamond Hill. The school, being a new school at the time of Glue's application, did not require applicants to be proficient in a musical instrument. All they wanted from the students was an average IELTS score of 5.5 or above and one year's tuition as a deposit. The school would invest the deposit into a fund and then return the amount to the family when the student graduated.

Whenever Glue practised the piano in his compartmentalized apartment (the four of them, Glue, Gwen, and their parents, shared a seven-hundred-square-foot space with two bedrooms), everyone else would retreat to their respective rooms and shut the doors. Nowadays, there is no piano in the apartment. Nowadays, Glue is alone. Nowadays, Gwen lives with her fiancé, Lester Tse. Glue's parents moved to Macau, for better benefits, after they retired.

**WHEN GLUE RETURNS** to his apartment, he tries to puke, can't, and decides to take a shower. He is alone, which is a good thing, because now he can take longer showers, and because he's alone, no one would find it odd that he laughs to himself in the shower. He does this quite often. He laughs as cold water runs down his back. The water in the shower takes a little less than a minute to get hot. He laughs for a minute or so, thinking about nothing, and when the water gets warm, he starts wondering what May could have possibly stolen from him.

*Stop thinking about what May stole.* Glue should be thinking about finding a job instead. He is beginning to feel financial pressure. Gwen is still paying part of the mortgage even though she's moved out, but Glue needs to pay his share. When he landed in Hong Kong six months back, he took on freelance gigs from a translation firm. He works from home, online, translating PR letters, translating up to five letters a day. But this gig, like most freelance translation gigs, is not stable. At least two days out of the week, Glue does not receive any assignments.

Gwen works full-time, has been working full-time for some time, and her connections are why Glue gets an interview with a school in Shenzhen. Glue needs to prepare himself, mentally, for the interview, which is necessary because he has been spending too much time alone, at home, laughing to himself in the shower; tomorrow's interview is the opposite of laughing in the shower. Glue will need to be a good communicator with good manners. Though Glue is aware of his need to focus, to think about the interview, one cannot control what one thinks about in the shower. So Glue thinks about what he knows about May—very little. They met on Tinder, matched less so because they were attracted to each other than because they both lived in the same neighbourhood. Up until a week ago, they had been having sex regularly, at least once every week. May likes being on top. Glue prefers being on the bottom. She, like Glue, lives alone in Tung Chung Crescent. Though they have a similar view, of the Ngong Ping mountain, May's place is much bigger. She lives in the penthouse. The duplex has two floors, three bedrooms, a washroom in the master bedroom on the second floor and another on the first floor for guests. May does not have a cat. Glue's neighbours, a Korean couple, have a cat, but most people in this compound do not have cats. Glue thinks this is a rule. *Domestic animals are not permitted on the premises of Tung Chung Crescent.* Glue has never seen this rule written down anywhere. He thinks a little more about what May could have stolen from him. He also begins to wonder if May will be leaving Hong Kong soon.

**NOW**, out of the shower, Glue thinks about calling Elle, to tell her what happened with May. Glue calls Elle on WhatsApp. Elle doesn't pick up. Glue tries again on WeChat. Seldom does Elle pick up lately, but just a month ago, when Elle picked up more often, they would talk for twenty minutes or so and then fall into silence, which is perhaps one of the reasons why Elle stopped picking up. Elle is not responsible for Glue's happiness. Elle said this to Glue on the phone once, offhandedly, when Glue was trying to tell her that he feels lost in Hong Kong. Glue wonders if, during that phone call, when he was trying to tell her that being back in Hong Kong made him feel lost, he sounded accusatory as well. Was he, albeit consciously or not, trying to blame Elle for his feeling lost? Is this what caused Elle to tell him that she is not responsible for his happiness? Is this why Elle opts to not pick up the phone when he calls?

But Elle is right. Glue is twenty-six—an adult. No one

should be responsible for his happiness anymore. Not his parents. Not Elle. Not May. Not Gwen.

Glue is beginning to feel as though May (not Elle) is doing him a favour. The feeling of feeling as if something you never noticed was yours is no longer yours, the feeling of losing ownership over something that you never knew you had ownership over, is a feeling that is preparing Glue, psychologically, for what is to come tomorrow because at the interview tomorrow, Gwen's former boss will have a conversation with Glue about his ability to comply with rules that Glue never knew existed. Glue will feel grateful to May for preparing him.

Glue first heard about this acquaintance of Gwen's when the siblings were still students in Canada. It was summer and the two were visiting their parents in Hong Kong. Gwen was telling Glue about someone she knew back when she was interning at a mid-sized consultancy firm. "He was my boss. Well, technically speaking, he was the director of the department, so he was my boss's boss? I forget what his position is exactly. He's Chinese, but grew up in Australia and the UK. He speaks a little Cantonese," Gwen said. "Not too well, though. The Cantonese of a third-grader, I guess."

This former boss's boss of Gwen's was afraid of "woke politics" and "cancel culture," so afraid that he decided to move to Hong Kong, where he felt there would be less of a chance that he would be cancelled. What Gwen did was something Glue could never do: expressed all the reasons why this man decided to move here as fact. Gwen's perfectly diplomatic cadence was without judgment, and Glue, when he heard all of this, felt something almost akin to sympathy.

*THE NEXT DAY*, Glue is on a high-speed train, heading to Shenzhen. The audiobook he's listening to usually pauses automatically when other apps play on Glue's phone but now that Glue is scrolling through Instagram with his VPN turned on and the internet connection is sometimes unstable when his VPN is on, the Instagram Reel's audio overlaps with that of the audiobook's. A promo for a Netflix special plays on Instagram and Pete Davidson is talking about how once, in the nineties, when he was babysitting while high on shrooms, the three-year-old boy started sucking on the comedian's finger while the two were watching *Forensic Files* and, at the same time, on Glue's audiobook, Marina Abramović is reading her memoir and it was the eighties and Abramović is talking about performing *Rest Energy* and about how fast her heart was beating and how the microphone was pressed against her heart when she held the bow and Ulay held the string and the arrow was pointing right against her chest—her heart. She wrote about how loud and fast their heartbeats were at that moment. The audience watched in silence, listening to their heartbeat, but then the audience burst out into laughter as Pete says that for a moment it felt good, having his finger sucked by the baby.

Glue thinks for a moment about his time commuting to work in Toronto and how he didn't even get cell phone reception on the subway half the time. He also thinks about what May could have possibly stolen from him. The fabric of his suit, a gift from his father for completing his undergrad, tailor-made by an old man in Sham Shui Po, is so hard Glue feels as though he is wearing cardboard. In Kowloon, it is hot and humid as usual, yet this air-conditioned high-speed train is cool, and almost immediately Glue's skin, once moist, becomes dehydrated once more as he enters the station, and now a thin layer of grease that is an amalgamation of Glue's sweat and oil emitted from his skin sits between his flesh and his cardboard suit. Though Glue is uncomfortable in this suit, this feeling, the feeling of having dried sweat on his body, is a feeling that Glue invites. This is the only suit he owns. If he dies, he will probably be laid in his casket in this suit. Glue thinks about dying some more. He often thinks about dying but never does he think much of how he would like to die. He imagines the feeling of having an arrow piercing through his heart and how good that would feel. Glue imagines Elle holding the string as he holds the bow. Glue leans back into his seat.

Elle would never do such a thing for Glue. Why would she? Elle is not responsible for his happiness. Would May hold the bow? No. May stole something from Glue. Perhaps Gwen would like to kill Glue. Gwen would probably enjoy killing Glue, Glue thinks. But *Rest Energy* should not be performed with Gwen. There is something intensely sexual in *Rest Energy*, something akin to true love. Gwen is, in a conventional way, a good sister. So good, in fact, that the lives of everyone in his family, Glue sometimes thinks, would be much simpler without him. His parents would probably be happier. This is not a sad thing but a realization, a simple fact that Glue accepted long ago. And long ago, Glue decided that there is little he can do to make life easier for Gwen and his parents.

But Glue still accepted this interview, and now he is remembering, or rather telling himself, that this is an interview he should take seriously because Gwen's name is on the line. Though Glue is qualified for the job on paper, he lacks the networking skills required to score an interview at this prestigious institution. Still, it is perhaps better if Gwen were to kill Glue. That would be much simpler.

*BUT THAT* won't happen. In twenty minutes, the high-speed rail takes Glue from Kowloon to Shenzhen North Station.

It takes him another ten minutes to get through customs.

An electric car that has green doors and looks like a toaster comes to pick Glue up. Glue, a Cantonese speaker, a Hong Konger who lived in Canada for eight years, has an odd accent when he's speaking Mandarin. Glue tells the driver where to stop. Gwen gave Glue clear instructions as to where to get off. "There's lots of construction. The government is trying to turn the area into an innovation park. You'll need to walk. The roads are narrow. Try to have the driver drop you off at the entrance to the area."

"How'd you know all of this?"

"Lester wanted to rent an office near there." Gwen kept her answer short.

The manager, in a pale pink shirt, navy suit, and Burberry belt, puts on his Dolce & Gabbana glasses, takes a glance at Glue's résumé, and says, "So, Glen Wu. Would you please tell me about yourself?"

In middle school, his friends started calling him "Glue" and the name has been stuck with him ever since.

Before Glue can reply, the man tells him that when he was young, he moved from Australia to England to teach Chinese and that he started becoming interested in the language at a young age because he grew up near Sydney's Chinatown. *"Became interested in the language?" Why is this man speaking as though he is not Chinese? And why is there a framed Rorschach inkblot hanging behind this guy?*

The man continues talking, compliments Gwen and notes that he is excited to meet his hardworking former intern's younger brother. "I'd like to get something clear before we move on, Glen. Let's address the elephant in the room."

"Sure."

"As you know, we're an English-speaking school in mainland China."

Glue nods.

"There are rules in mainland China. Since you're a Hong Konger who studied in Canada, you need to be doubly cautious. You must know this already but both places you are associated with do not exactly have a great relationship with China right now. This is an apolitical school, and we'd like to keep it that way."

"Of course."

"I don't know about you, Glen, but I feel quite comfortable here. I think it might be good that there are certain parameters in place that let students focus on learning. All the conversations about race and politics and rights are distracting sometimes. We shouldn't be talking about things we can't really change right now." He takes a sip from his tumbler, which has his initials engraved on its surface. "Can you imagine saying such a thing in the West? Here, though, saying such things is considered politically correct. Am I right? Interesting, isn't it?"

These words do not trigger Glue. Because of this, the rest of the interview is alright because Glue bears with him the feeling that something of his is gone. Everything can be gone at any given moment. Nothing belongs to Glue. There's no point in being triggered.

On the way back to the station, hearing Glue's accent, the driver asks if he is Korean. Glue tells him that he is not, and the driver asks Glue if he is Japanese. Glue tells him that he is not but, remembering what the manager had said, he does not tell the driver that he came from Hong Kong and studied in Canada. The driver tells Glue that if he is Japanese, he will kick him out. They are on a highway. Glue glimpses a slight smirk on the driver's face in the rear-view mirror. Glue remembers that when he was ten or eleven or twelve, he watched as a girl he liked drew a cat, a small cat with small eyes and small ears and a tiny tail, and when Glue returned home from school, and he didn't realize he was doing this until he did it, he imagined he was her, the girl he liked, as he drew the same cat, and he imagined that the cat was alive, and he imagined strangling the cat, just enough to make it sense death before setting it free.

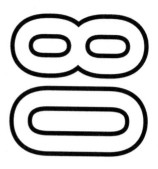

**ON HIS WAY HOME**, on the MTR from Kowloon station to Tung Chung, as he passes by thousands of shipping containers in the terminal between Nam Cheong station and Lai King station, Glue scrolls through his phone. He sees an email from the University of Toronto telling him that the deadline to reactivate his email account is tonight.

Deadline? This tickles Glue's mind. The word "deadline" strikes Glue as extremely odd. Why is this word allowed to combine time, space, life, action, and urgency into one clear idea? It seems unfair. Sometimes, the meanings of words escape Glue. He recalls the time when as a teen, in order to successfully transfer to an international school, he spent hours preparing for the speaking portion of the IELTS exam. He listened to hundreds of speeches by past American presidents. The IELTS test is expensive, Glue knew, so he studied hard, listened to speeches at night when he slept, and, when he couldn't sleep, he played Obama's speeches in the background as he browsed through videos on Pornhub. Many times, he ejaculated to videos of strangers fucking and the deep yet soothing voice of the forty-fourth US president. He passed the test, of course, but some marks were taken off because he paused too much in the middle of his sentences, which he sometimes still does when he's nervous.

Glue will not remember to reactivate his email tonight. Slowly, his years spent in Canada will fade away. Soon, his missing Elle, and wondering what May stole, will also fade. But that time has yet to come. At this moment, thinking about the word "deadline" makes Glue wonder if May will be leaving soon. The thought of May leaving makes his heart beat fast. He thinks about texting May but doesn't.

Glue, in this air-conditioned train that will take him back to Lantau Island, feels that emptiness is creeping inside him. From the Tung Chung Line's smooth silver seats made of aluminum, this emptiness enters his anus, creeps up his rectum, and makes its way through everything inside him until it reaches his heart. This is not the first time. He has felt this feeling before, when he asked Elle to move in with him.

Glue had called Elle. "Gwen's going to be away."

"What?"

"She wants to tell you that—"

Gwen grabbed the phone from Glue. "Elle! Sorry, I wanted to tell you myself. I got the internship in Dubai! I'll be leaving in a few weeks. And Glue wants to talk to you."

"Gwen's going back to Hong Kong after her internship," Glue said, his voice cracking a little, "so it looks like she won't be coming back to Toronto anytime soon." Glue paused. "Maybe, I was thinking, you should move in with me."

*GLUE TRIES* to call Elle when he gets home. Elle still isn't picking up. Elle is in Singapore. It is 8:29 p.m. on a Wednesday. Elle, who usually goes out for drinks on Thursdays, should be at home with her parents, who complain whenever she spends less than three days a week having dinner at home. At 8:30, Elle is usually on her phone, chilling on the couch. Glue checks Elle's Instagram story—no new updates. Before, Elle had blocked Glue on all her social media, but after they went their separate ways, Elle back to Singapore and Glue back to Hong Kong, Elle added Glue back on all her social media. The last time she tweeted was this morning, a retweet of a tweet about a *New Yorker* article on the mysteries of business casual. Elle doesn't tweet much. She studied fashion and her mother owns a fashion boutique in Singapore. Most of her tweets are just retweets of fashion articles.

The article Elle retweeted this morning looks, from a socio-anthropological perspective, at the recent trend of Wall Street elites switching to Ray-Bans and synthetic wool fleece vests instead of three-piece suits—a trend, the article states, that is indicative of late modern capitalism. Glue recalls seeing the same phenomenon on Hong Kong Island, in Central, at the IFC, where, on the long pedestrian bridges that connect the Hong Kong MTR station and the offices above to Central, European men and local finance bros alike sport similar outfits in the winter. Because of this, Glue finds this article relatable, which is a good thing because in more ways than one, the goal of Hong Kong, we all know, because of its history of trade (and colonization), is to become the New York City of Asia.

With its financial infrastructure, Hong Kong is the rest of the world's gateway to China. To China, Hong Kong is a Chinese city that can rival the likes of New York City. Central, thus, is Asia's Wall Street. But there is more. Glue, being raised in Hong Kong, knows that proximity is everything. Silicon Valley is too far from New York City. Shenzhen, on the other hand, is Hong Kong's neighbouring city and Asia's tech hub. The home of Huawei and Tencent, Shenzhen rivals Silicon Valley's tech scene and is supposed to lead the world in innovation. And then there is Macau, *the Las Vegas of the East*. The south of China is designed to encompass some of the most important traits of the American Empire. Because of all this, Glue feels a homely warmth reading this *New Yorker* article about how people dress in New York City retweeted by his Singaporean Chinese ex-girlfriend.

But this sense of familiarity also makes Glue feel alienated. The Hong Kong portrayed in the *Financial Times*, the Hong Kong that is Wall Street–like, is not the Hong Kong in which he belongs. The finance bro's updated uniform, a Patagonia vest worn atop a light blue long-sleeve designer shirt, is a symbol of male corporate power at the elite level; the Hong Kong Island business casual is a language of power. Glue does not own anything of the sort. His closet consists of simple T-shirts from Zara and Nike shorts bought at a discount at the Nike outlet at the mall downstairs in Tung Chung. Glue continues scrolling through the article and learns that Patagonia works only with companies whose environmental and social values reflect its own. This, like most fashion trends, aims to exclude, raising the "ethical" finance bros—the capitalists with a sense of social-environmental awareness—above the didactic capitalists, the cringey ones with three-piece suits and ties.

*ELLE NEVER CRITICIZED* how Glue dressed; remembering this gives Glue a sense of comfort. Reading this article, he recalls yet another conversation with Elle.

"I'll feel guilty living in Hong Kong as a foreigner." Glue remembers Elle telling him this at a Second Cup. There were cookie crumbs and coffee stains on the table. "I don't want to live there again." Elle's father had relocated to Hong Kong for work when she was fifteen. Elle spent the first two years of high school at an international school before returning to Singapore.

But Elle was right, Glue knew. Hong Kong is a place where you would want to live only if you had the option to leave.

"So," Glue had to ask, "if I choose to return to Hong Kong, would we break up?"

"I'm not sure yet," Elle said.

There was never a formal breakup. Instead, Elle picked up Glue's calls less frequently after the two went back home.

Glue goes on YouTube. He remembers when he and Elle were in Toronto, lying in bed, high. They had just finished watching the movie *Ponyo* (2008), a Miyazaki anime about a goldfish who escapes the ocean and falls in love with a boy. They watched the film on Glue's laptop, on a Chinese website with Chinese subtitles. The subtitles were perfect. There were even footnotes to explain the cultural references in the film that otherwise would have been lost in translation. Glue remembers admiring the effort Chinese hackers put into making foreign content available to mainland Chinese audiences. When the film ended, Elle clicked one of the pop-up ads and another film started playing. Three people, two men and one woman, were setting up a campsite. The camp setting was so detailed. One character read the instructions in the tent manual to another. After five minutes or so, when the tent was set up and it had begun to turn dark, one of the characters started a fire. The three roasted marshmallows.

Glue remembers that Elle felt his groin. Glue, for some reason, was hard, and the two started laughing. Glue tried dragging the bar forward to get to the action, but after the roasting of marshmallows, the three, who were supposed to fuck, simply started reading in the tent.

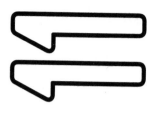

**GLUE IS WATCHING** a *Democracy Now!* video on the toilet. There's something about the Hong Kong protest and something about Facebook trying to digitize currency. There's police violence in America. Glue stops watching the video. Glue cannot shit.

He gives up trying to shit. He thinks about drawing a cat. He doesn't draw a cat. He checks his phone. Elle has yet to respond to his call. He wonders what May stole from him. He starts going through the things he thinks might be worth stealing in his bedroom. The stash he got from Po-Wing is still tucked under the bed, the stack of cash in a mooncake box is in his underwear drawer, and the orange butt plug is also under his bed. Everything is where it's supposed to be. He checks the login history on all his social media accounts—nothing unusual. He does not have a high limit on his HSBC Visa card, but still, he checks his transactions—nothing suspicious.

He checks his bank balance and, looking at the small

amount he has in his savings account, feels ridiculous. May would not steal money. May is not strapped for cash. On paper, the cryptocurrency firm May works for is a London-based company. It was created by Chinese entrepreneurs and none of the employees live in the UK. Though each employee has a standard monthly salary, the reason May works at this company is that, in addition to the base salary, everyone is paid nontaxable bonuses, in different types of crypto, every few months.

Glue feels as if his entire body is stuck in time. His bowels are not moving. Glue hasn't been exercising much and has been eating at McDonald's way too often. Glue only started eating at McDonald's after he returned to Hong Kong. When he was in Toronto, Glue and Elle would go out for tacos. Glue would stand in line at Seven Lives to get tacos for the two of them while Elle searched for vintage goods in Kensington Market. Glue still recalls feeling the taco grease seeping through the flimsy butcher's wrap as he walked towards Elle.

Now Glue is standing in the living room, staring out the window at the mountains. He returns to the toilet. Nope, still can't shit.

"Constipation" sounds a little like "simulation," which reminds Glue of the word "assimilation," and the word "assimilation" makes him think about the sex he's been having with May for the past months. She's always the one who initiates, who comes over to his place, knowing exactly what she wants. Glue enjoys how little control he has when she's on top, riding him. She puts a blindfold on him and ties his arms to the bed. She often slaps him and even chokes him without warning. This lack of agency is the freedom Glue actively invites.

Glue is hard. Constipation, arousal, confusion, a looming sense of depression, and a vague sense of loss are all coming together naturally.

便秘 (bin[6] bei) is "constipation"; 便 on its own means "easy," "informal," "ordinary," and "comfort." 秘, on the other hand, means "secret." The words 便秘 describe this moment better than any English word Glue knows.

He stands up and ejaculates into some toilet paper and approaches something like a state of post-nut clarity: There is no point waiting to hear back from the school in Shenzhen, Glue feels. He knows he won't get the job. Glue considers becoming an ESL instructor.

"Teaching ESL is as stable a career as someone like you can have." Glue remembers a FaceTime conversation he had with his mother earlier in the week. Glue's mom calls this 馬死落地行 (direct translation: "When the horse dies, walk on your feet," a more—utilitarian?—way of saying "suck it up"). "I mean, you've never even had a full-time job. It's about time."

**GLUE'S FIRST-EVER** paid job was at Hong Kong Disneyland. Summer is when international students return to their home countries to spend time with their families and, sometimes, work. Back then, Glue was, above all things, a depressed nineteen-year-old drama student coming home to Hong Kong's humid summer. He was developing a liking for whiskey and had read *The Communist Manifesto* for the first time. He'd read plays by Beckett and other books translated from the French—the writings of Albert Camus, Simone Weil, and Frantz Fanon. Though Glue didn't understand much of what he was reading, Fanon's sentences felt important, and this was enough to convince Glue to continue exploring his works that summer.

This was also the summer Glue began working. He had a summer position as a media coordinator working for a producer at Disneyland. The hourly rate was hefty. The producer was a childhood friend of his mother's, which is why he got the position. "No problem," the producer said.

"It's hard to get a job in the arts, especially in Hong Kong. We need young people like you, Glen Wu. Just work hard. There's no need to thank me." But before he began to work, Glue had to attend training sessions. For five days straight, every new employee had to learn about the ideology of Disney. The corporation redefined "happiness" for their workers and gave anecdotes about working-class families who saved up for months just so they could bring their children to Disneyland for a day. But what would Walt Disney think about a bunch of chinks walking around on his property? This ideology, Glue knew, was all empty rhetoric that ignored how Disney has produced Orientalist films and Disneyland itself has gentrified the shit out of a bunch of places—but Glue wanted the money. Glue tried not to quit.

Halfway through the week of brainwashing camp, Glue started drinking in the bathroom during breaks. He couldn't handle being sober while listening to lectures about the Disney spirit. Thank God, Glue, on his way to work, was able to buy whiskey at the 7-Eleven near his place, and thanks to the cheap whiskey, he was able to bear sitting through a week of bullshit. The Disney logo depressed Glue, and seeing Mickey Mouse walking around in the humid summer, his costume red and black and white, reminded him of the symbols used by certain right-wing groups. Even after he began his job as a media coordinator, Glue continued taking sips from the small bottle of Johnnie Walker he kept in his bag. He did this despite feeling constantly dehydrated in Hong Kong's steaming heat. His face was often red and greasy, and having BB cream on his face made Glue feel as if a layer of his skin were melting off.

When Glue was in his teens, his classmates made fun of his pimpled face. His black-framed glasses fell to the tip of his nose whenever he sweated. He had a chin that was too close to his neck, and imperfect teeth. If only Glue had worn contact lenses back then (and had gotten some dental work done), he would have looked better. But because Glue's mother also believed that contact lenses were harmful to one's eyes, especially for teenagers, Glue spent those years looking like a greasy-faced camel with glasses.

At Disneyland, nineteen-year-old Glue looked better. Though his teeth were still imperfect, he had more muscle. He also had on contact lenses. In the smothering heat, however, Glue felt as if his contact lenses were melting into his eyeballs.

"You okay?" said the producer, patting Glue on his shoulder.

"I'm good."

"We'll be meeting here at nine tomorrow. Make sure you're here on time, okay?"

Glue was to escort a film crew to different locations in the park to shoot a segment for an afternoon talk show.

That night, knowing that he could not be late, Glue tried to sleep early. He went to bed at nine thirty, got on Pornhub, and by ten he had masturbated himself to sleep while watching an interracial threesome, but two hours later, at midnight, Glue found himself awake, on his phone, sitting on the toilet with the lights turned off, the sound of the exhaust fan buzzing in his ears as he read about the recent controversies Disney was involved in. A woman had filed a federal lawsuit against the Walt Disney Company because her supervisor prohibited her from wearing her headscarf to work. She also claimed that her co-workers and supervisors accosted her with anti-Muslim slurs, calling her "terrorist," "camel," and "Kunta Kinte."

Glue, when he finished reading the article, in the darkness of the washroom, found himself at work. "We welcome all cultures here at Hong Kong Disneyland. So, to resolve concerns over hijabs falling off our patrons' heads when they are enjoying our rides, we now offer this device." The producer, decked out in full suit and tie in the blistering heat, took out a black bag with two eyeholes. "Now, regardless of where you are from or what your beliefs are, you can enjoy *all* the rides here at the Happiest Place on Earth. After all, in Hong Kong, there is religious freedom."

Glue watched as the television host, with a black bag over her head, flew by on the rollercoaster.

After, when the host, panting, took the bag off her face, the director said to her, "That's no good. You gotta look more excited. We're in Disneyland! Come on. Let's do one more!"

The next time around, perhaps to act excited, the host raised both hands in the dirty air, which made it look like she was surrendering, bag still covering her face. It was 35°C that day.

Glue, witnessing this bizarre event, felt dizzy. He was sweating through his white shirt, and his collar was stained with the BB cream that he put on his face that morning. He vomited his breakfast all over the floor. For a moment he felt relieved, as though a ghost that lived inside him had disappeared. But the comfort didn't last. A moment later, Glue felt his head buzzing and his throat drying. He wanted water but there was no sink in this washroom. He felt his head becoming lighter and lighter. He woke in his bed to his phone ringing. "You there, Glen Wu? The crew is waiting for you." It was the producer. "I was told to check on you. Did you get lost or something? Hurry up. We only have one day with these guys."

Glue checked his phone. It was nine in the morning. Did he not finish the shoot? Did Glue, after reading the news article, drink a half-bottle of whiskey and pass out at home? Glue got up, felt woozy from getting up too quickly, and vomited on the floor. At this moment, he felt as if his stomach were the world and the world were bursting.

Glue did not make it to work that day. The next day, he was fired.

GLUE'S MOTHER WAS EMBARRASSED, of course, having learned that her son had been drinking the entire time he was on the job she'd gotten for him using her connections.

"It's okay. This job is not for everyone." The producer seemed forgiving, but Glue's mother would have none of it. Though they lived in the same apartment, Glue's mother did not speak to Glue for the remainder of the summer. Gwen, who had an internship with the government, would try to talk to Glue despite being exhausted from her job, but Glue preferred to retreat to his room.

If only Glue were stronger back then, had that able-to-walk-on-two-legs-if-the-horse-dies mentality, he would have gone back the following summer, and now he would have a full-time job at Hong Kong Disneyland. But he didn't. For the rest of that summer, he would drink from the bottle of Johnnie Walker he hid under his bed and walk around the neighbourhood alone at night. Sometimes, his childhood best friend, Po-Wing, would join him.

Unlike Glue, Po-Wing did not even attempt to get a summer job. On the side, he dealt weed. "Unlike you wealthy assholes, my parents don't care if I work in the summer or not. They're just happy I got into Kong U and that I'm getting a degree. I don't think they even know what my major is."

Thinking about failing at his first job makes Glue retreat to the bathroom. He still can't shit. He goes on YouTube. The user Oriental Pearl appears on his home page. "You speak fluent Chinese and Japanese. You're learning some Korean. You must catch people talking about you, right?" says Oriental Pearl, a white woman with blond hair, standing in the middle of the streets of Tokyo. "I caught people talking about me in Chinese and Japanese. See what their reactions are when I tell them I understood everything they said."[1]

Being able to articulate the feeling of feeling as though people are talking about you and being able to express that feeling because you feel safe enough to film a YouTube video is bullshit, Glue thinks. Glue is certain that if someone does start talking about him, he will certainly not feel safe enough to film it.

---

1

Glue closes YouTube on his phone. He has the sudden urge to get high. Should he call Po-Wing? No. It is not yet time to get high. It is time to make a decision. Glue, at this moment, decides that he will become an ESL instructor.

The decision of becoming an ESL instructor is made, Glue feels as though he has done enough today.

*Now* it is time to get high.

# OCEAN

二

SHIT

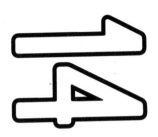

**NOW**, at Po-Wing's apartment, in Po-Wing's washroom, Glue is imagining a sea of turtles, walking backwards back into the ocean, but his dick remains hard. In an American sitcom he once saw (was it *How I Met Your Mother?*), a middle-aged white guy, to last longer, would think about turtles when he's about to cum. Turtles calm his dick down; Glue's is still stiff. How did it get so hard? He takes a piss. He can't find a hand towel anywhere in this tiny washroom but notices a shiny silver hand dryer near the door. It's a Dyson Airblade AB14. Glue has seen this hand dryer at airports, office buildings, and train stations but never in a person's apartment. According to Google, it costs around HK$7,000. Glue puts his hands inside the AB14. As the warm air runs over his fingers, his dick starts stiffening, and when his hands are finally dry, Glue becomes fully erect.

Glue's dick feels even harder than usual because he's high. Do hand dryers do it for Glue? To combat this seemingly unprovoked arousal, Glue thinks about corn. He read, recently, a story by a Korean writer suggested to him by Amazon's algorithm. The story opens with a vignette about a man who thinks he's a cob of corn. The man's doctor manages to convince him that he is a human being, not corn. So the man is dispatched from the facility. But not long after, he returns.

"Help!" the man says. "The chickens are after me!"

"You're not a cob of corn anymore, remember?" the doctor replies.

"I know that, but the chickens don't."

The rest of the story is about a writer and has nothing to do with corn. But this corn man, not anything else, is all Glue can think about right now.

And now, a small tent is forming, raising the length of Glue's black Nike gym shorts a few more centimetres above his knees. Glue sits on the toilet. *I'm a cob of corn.* He mouths the words, doesn't just think them. *I am a cob of corn. I am a cob of corn.*

Po-Wing knocks on the door. "Yo. You okay?"

"There's a hand dryer in your washroom," Glue says.

"You like it?" Po-Wing asks. "It was a gift. Pretty nice, yeah?"

Do people give hand dryers as gifts?

Po-Wing has a chin-up bar attached to his bedroom door. He's doing reps. The bedroom door is left open. His double bed is unmade; socks, underwear, and designer shopping bags lie all over the floor. He pulls himself up as in front of him, an episode of *SpongeBob Square Pants* plays on his Samsung 65" 4K UHD HDR Curved LED Tizen Smart TV. The Beolab 18 home theatre set by Bang & Olufsen—which looks incredibly stylish but entirely out of place in this four-hundred-square-foot government-subsidized apartment—is turned off.

Panting, Po-Wing sits down on the couch, next to Glue, and chugs an entire bottle of Evian before rolling a joint. Sweat slides down the side of his face as he licks the rolling paper with the tip of his tongue and gently folds it together with the tips of his fingers. He lights the thick joint between his lips, and slowly, he exhales.

"SpongeBob is one of America's finest exports," Po-Wing says as he passes Glue the joint.

Glue nods. Not knowing what to say to that, Glue takes a drag and gives SpongeBob a dirty look. *One of America's finest exports, huh?* Perhaps there's some truth to that. Here they are, two Chinese dudes, getting high in a government-subsidized apartment in Tung Chung, watching this show about a yellow sponge who lives in a pineapple under the sea on a 65" Samsung TV with the B&O speakers turned off.

"Can I have some water?" Glue asks Po-Wing.

Po-Wing tosses him a bottle of Evian. "Your sister—what's up with her? She moved out from your apartment already?"

"Yeah, a month or so ago," Glue says, still staring at the yellow sponge.

Po-Wing's eyes are now fixed on the commercials: a commercial for *La La Land*—now available in Blu-ray.

"You've seen *La La Land*?" Po-Wing asks Glue.

"Yeah, when I was in Toronto."

"They told you you'd have more opportunities with a foreign degree, didn't they? How many degrees do you have again? Two?"

Glue nods. After graduating from the University of Toronto with a drama degree, he spent a year in teachers' college at York University before starting (but not finishing) an MFA in creative writing.

"Yo, Glue. Fast food restaurants are cheap. You know why?" Po-Wing asks, staring at the McDonald's commercial on his curved TV, jittering his right leg. Without waiting for Glue's response, Po-Wing tells Glue, "They sell us cheap shit to keep us full and so unhealthy so that we won't start a class war." Po-Wing laughs. "Genius, right?"

Glue just continues to smoke his joint.

"*SpongeBob* is created by a marine scientist, you know." Po-Wing says this matter-of-factly.

Glue nods. This weed tastes like ass (in a bad way). Glue knows that smoking this will probably give him a heavy hangover. But he takes another drag. It's hard to get good weed in Hong Kong, and all Glue wants is to get high.

Glue's head feels numb, and his eyes are reddening.

"Here." Po-Wing tosses Glue a small bottle of Rohto Lycée Blanc Heart-Shaped Eye Drops from his pocket. "The Japanese make the best eye drops," Po-Wing says. Opening his eyes wide, Po-Wing gives Glue a huge smile, showing his perfect teeth.

Glue still looks like he has a double chin at times. When he was a teenager he was advised by his dentist to get braces, which would have elongated his chin a little, giving him a more pronounced jawline, but Glue never got the braces. Glue's mother thought the braces were too expensive. "It's not like you're going to be a celebrity, Glen Wu. Save some money." Glue also does this weird thing with his mouth whenever he applies eye drops: he tilts his head up, opens his eyes as wide as possible, and, as the droplet falls, he twists his jaw away from the rest of his face. This, combined with the close proximity between his chin and neck, makes it look as if the lower half of Glue's face is being sucked in by the space around him.

"You look like a Picasso painting," Po-Wing says. "Come on. We're going for a drive."

Po-Wing takes off his black Comme des Garçons Play T-shirt, smells it, and tosses it on the couch on top of a pile of other shirts—all designer labels, all imports: Sacai, Balenciaga, Givenchy, Valentino, Moschino. Po-Wing pulls one out from the pile, a green piqué polo shirt, and puts it on over his Nike x Off-White shorts.

*THE AIR*, so humid that you can gargle it in your mouth, smothers Glue's skin the moment he leaves Po-Wing's air-conditioned apartment. Po-Wing's apartment building is hideous. All the windows are barred, and the tiles on the floor crisscross in shades of light green and white. When in the history of Hong Kong did we think that this was a good look?

"These buildings are durable, though, look the same now compared to twenty years ago," Po-Wing says, without looking at Glue.

Each apartment has two doors, the wooden one that comes with the flat and a barred iron gate installed in front. Some of the wooden doors are left open. Glue hears noises from televisions. Next to some of the doors are red boards, around two feet high, with the words "地主" (Earth God) written in glittery gold. Red electric candles, in the shape of flames, illuminate each of the boards. Glue smells incense burning.

Though the parking lot smells musty, and the ground is unpaved, with puddles everywhere, all the cars are spotless. Is that a Maserati?

"She rarely drives that one," Po-Wing tells Glue. "It's my neighbour's. She likes that one more." He points at a black 2018 Lexus hybrid SUV. "I bet there are more sports cars here than at that middle-class private housing complex of yours. Living in public housing saves you tons."

Po-Wing's Tesla Model 3 is red. He turns on his autopilot, lowers the windows, and lights a cigarette. It is 2 a.m. The two of them are the only ones leaving Lantau Island. Glue reaches his hand out the window to feel the breeze. As the hot current runs through Glue's fingers, just like the Dyson Airblade did, his dick starts getting hard again. *I am a cob of corn.*

"What'd you say?"

"What?"

"You said something."

"You . . . um . . . mind if we play some music?" Glue never wants to listen to music.

"No. I don't have a phone anymore, so you'll need to use yours," Po-Wing says.

Why doesn't he have a phone?

"I do have a phone. Duh. I just don't have a smartphone anymore. I have a flip phone now. It's a Nokia Go Flip 3." Po-Wing takes it out from his pocket and flips it open.

They get off the highway and enter the Cheung Ching Tunnel before getting on the Tsing Sha Highway.

"We're going to Container Terminal 8 West," Po-Wing answers before Glue even asks. "You should leave your phone in the car when we get there."

"Do I have to?"

Commercial goods from abroad enter through this terminal. Thousands of cargo containers, in red, blue, and green, stack on top of each other. Glue feels small.

Po-Wing hands Glue a flashlight from his frunk. The cargo terminal is between the Rambler Channel, which connects to the South China Sea, and Stonecutters Island. They walk away from the sea, towards the hills. It is perfectly dark and quiet. Glue hears birds chirping as he walks closer to the hills.

"Here we are," Po-Wing says, after twenty minutes or so. Standing in front of them is a white Guanyin statue, nearly eight metres tall. What is this doing here? She looks down at them with her gentle face. Her eyes are closed, and in her right hand, she holds a perfectly round sphere, and in her left, she holds a thin bottle. The tip of the bottle is pointing down at Glue and Po-Wing. Glue's penis, fully erect at this point, is pointing right back at the Guanyin. This must be incredibly disrespectful, but is it really Glue's fault? Guanyin would understand. Besides, who is Glue to combat this natural phenomenon?

"I come here sometimes," Po-Wing says. He lights another joint from his pocket, his third of the night. They smoke again. They exhale at the Guanyin's face. Weed might be illegal in Hong Kong, but the Guanyin doesn't care. "I come here. I smoke, and then I head the other way, towards the Rambler Channel. It's good, it helps me clear my mind. I do this once every two months or so. This is the first time I brought someone with me, Glue."

Glue wants to ask Po-Wing why he brought him here but starts feeling his tongue turning numb.

"It's kind of like a ritual for me," Po-Wing says, "coming here to smoke with her."

Po-Wing finishes the joint and starts walking in the other direction, towards the ocean.

Glue, so high he can barely continue walking, lets his dick remain erect. Glue finds himself standing alone at the edge of the pier. They had finished smoking under the Guanyin and started walking in this direction, through the cargoes. And? What happened after? Glue cannot recall. His pockets are empty. His phone and his keys are in Po-Wing's car. Po-Wing is nowhere to be seen. All that he is left with is the cheap white linen T-shirt from Zara he has on, black Nike gym shorts, and a hard-on.

What should Glue do? Glue thinks for a moment. There's no one around. So he reaches inside his shorts and cups his balls with his palm. It feels warm. He does this for some time, caressing his testicles. Po-Wing is nowhere in sight. Surely, Po-Wing would not leave Glue stranded in this cargo terminal. All Glue needs to do is to stay here until Po-Wing comes back for him. After reassuring himself, he whips his cock out. Facing the ocean, he starts stroking his dick, each stroke a little faster than the last. He keeps his eyes open, as wide as possible, gazing at the darkness of the ocean. He starts smiling, showing all of his teeth and staring at the black sea, and, thinking about nothing in particular, Glue ejaculates.

Lights are flickering behind him, the Tesla's headlights, probably. Po-Wing gives Glue a soft honk, but Glue doesn't turn around. He needs a moment. Po-Wing turns the radio on. Glue continues stroking his rock-hard cock. Glue hears, from the radio, a woman's voice, an advertisement for the new Samsung Galaxy S. The commercial is in Mandarin. Glue continues masturbating. The commercial ends. Po-Wing switches the channel. A familiar rhythm starts playing—a national anthem? At least it sounds like one. But which country's national anthem this is, Glue cannot tell, nor can he tell what language this anthem is in. Po-Wing honks. All Glue knows is that what he is hearing is a national anthem and that this music is, for some reason, making his prick even harder. Because it feels so good, Glue starts laughing a little as he continues to stroke his dick to the music. "I am a cob of corn," he mumbles, trying to make this moment last a bit longer.

Glue does this as discreetly as possible, hoping Po-Wing won't notice. Listening to the national anthem, he ejaculates, triumphantly, shamelessly, into the darkness of the sea.

**"YOU HUNGRY?"** Po-Wing hands Glue a bottle of Evian.

Glue nods and closes his eyes. The car comes to a stop.

"Yo. Get up, Glue. Let's eat."

Glue gets out of the Tesla and finds himself in the parking lot of the Hong Kong International Airport.

"Come on," says Po-Wing. They walk towards Terminal 1. It is almost four in the morning. How is Po-Wing, after having smoked so many joints, able to drive here? "Good thing we live near the airport, right?"

McDonald's in Hong Kong is probably the best in the world. When he's high Glue orders the GCB:[2] "Tender boneless chicken thigh seasoned with black pepper and grilled to perfection, served with fresh, crunchy lettuce and tasty chargrill sauce in a fluffy bun."

They walk past tourists, white backpackers with scruffy beards and greasy hair, charging their laptops, sleeping on the floor. Why do Westerners in Hong Kong prefer to sit on the floor rather than chairs? They sit on the floors on the subway, on platforms, on the ferries too.

Back in the parking lot, Po-Wing and Glue sit on the Tesla's hood and eat their sandwiches. Glue's back is sweaty. The sky is dark. They can hear, somewhere far away, a double-decker braking to a stop. Just hearing the braking noise makes Glue think of the reek of gasoline from the bottom of the bus.

Glue takes another bite of his sandwich. Nothing reminds him of scentless Canada.

**ALL GLUE** wants to do the next day, a Monday, a national holiday, is to get high, eat takeout alone at home, and watch a nine-minute highlight of an NBA game on YouTube. But it is July. The NBA season is over. Glue is having dinner with his family, in Macau, where his parents retired. The evening news is playing on the television. When Glue was growing up, the evening news added noise to the silence between Glue's parents and their children during dinner. Nothing ever changes. In this small apartment, the evening news underscores the conversation between Gwen Wu, Gwen's fiancé, Lester Tse, and Glue's parents. This is 電視撈飯 (direct translation: "rice mixed with television").

The news anchor says something about Trump and China. There's some news about North Korea as well. The prime minister of Japan visits the Yasukuni Shrine, again. Glue is the only one watching, his head slightly turned, facing the television, chewing his char siu while the TV flashes information in front of him. Glue really shouldn't be eating char siu because he will continue to be constipated. But char siu is soft and sweet and being able to enjoy chewing small pieces of barbecued meat glazed with honey is probably the best July First Glue could ask for.

"My friend's daughter," says Glue's dad, "she went to teachers' college. I think she even went to Columbia. She couldn't get a job in Hong Kong. But you know what? There're many students from mainland who want to go abroad these days. Immigration consultants, ESL instructors, these fields are booming. She's earning loads as an IELTS tutor now. You should get on to that soon, you know?"

This is the first time Glue's dad has said anything tonight. Glue's dad is often silent. Glue and Gwen think this is because speaking less makes him feel more powerful when he does speak.

Everyone but Gwen stares at Glue. Gwen continues to 扒飯 (the rapid motion of holding one's bowl close to one's face and using one's chopsticks to direct the rice into one's mouth). Knowing that Glue resents the ESL business, Gwen does not want any part of this. Glue, assuming he did not get the job in Shenzhen, has already decided to become an ESL instructor, though he hasn't told anyone yet. The news cycle doesn't care. The Alibaba Group's stock prices continue to rise. There's yet another protest. Pro-democracy activists in Hong Kong occupied the

Legislative Council Complex. Elon Musk is named the richest person alive, and Japan decides to dump one million tonnes of contaminated water from the Fukushima nuclear plant into the sea.

**BECAUSE GLUE** doesn't respond to Glue's dad, Lester Tse responds for him: "Yeah. It's messy here. People are looking to leave. It's funny that the three of us chose to come back. 回流."

回流 means "returning current." For overseas Chinese, moving to China is not a step forward in life but a step backwards; like salmon, Glue was just swimming around the ocean all his life only to return to the same place—China. All roads lead to China, as they say. One belt, one road.

回流. Lester Tse pronounces the phrase in Cantonese.

"Not bad," says Glue's dad. "Your Cantonese is getting better." Up until this point, they have been switching between English and Mandarin. Lester Tse is from Mississauga and learned Mandarin from his grandmother.

"There's no point learning Cantonese," Glue's mom says. "Lester is fluent in Mandarin. All you need is English and Mandarin." Glue's mom usually doesn't like

CBCs—Canadian-born Chinese. She thinks they're too privileged, too used to being able to say and do whatever they want, and that they use that to distinguish themselves from the Chinese Chinese. Back in the 2000s, Glue's mother would complain that Glue's cousins in Canada grew up under too little pressure. She also thinks CBCs are too simple-minded. They don't understand the "complex workings of Asia," she claimed: "Everything is either left or right, blue or red, good or bad in the West," she used to say. "Here, it's different, more complex, more history."

Glue, back then, was embarrassed by such comments from his mother. Glue thought his mother's comments contrived, as if lifted from a character in *The Joy Luck Club*. Now, though, after having moved back to Hong Kong, and since Lester Tse began joining family gatherings, Glue is considering his mother's comments on CBCs once more. Perhaps there is a part of him that longs to be ignorant of and free from the "complex workings of Asia," the circumstance he was born into. A part of him that wants to be oblivious. Orientalists are free. They live in their imaginations, fantastic projections of reality.

Glue sees a Colgate commercial on TV. A commercial for the new Huawei phone. A travel agency's new deals for trips to Kweilin and deals for hotel rooms at the Venetian, where there are indoor bridges and canals and where the ceiling is painted sky blue. In Macau, the job of broadcasting companies is not so much to produce content but to buy and redistribute shit. Why make cultural products of your own when mainland China, the US, the UK, the rest of Europe, as well as neighbouring countries such as Japan and Korea, throw so much more money into content production, Glue thinks. Just self-Orientalize and watch sitcoms. Watch *Friends* and *How I Met Your Mother*. Laugh when the Western studio audiences do. Watch *90210* and *Gossip Girl* (and, in two years, the *Gossip Girl* reboot). Live vicariously in New York. Copy their fashion. Read the poorly subbed subtitles. Learn English. If Marvel movies aren't for you, watch anime. Watch *Pokémon* and *Naruto*. The entirety of Studio Ghibli's body of work is available on Netflix and so is *Attack on Titan* and *Death Note*. Listen to K-pop. *BLACKPINK*! Think about the Kardashians more often. Watch Gordon Ramsay learn how to make pad thai from an old Thai lady whose name no one will remember.

Glue self-Orientalizes. Everyone does it. We're all guilty. Borrowing power from the powerful as a demonstration of cultural nationalism. Some do this to attract tourists. Some, like Elle and May, learn to speak English in a British accent. Growing up in Hong Kong in the early 2000s, Glue started learning English at the age of six so that he would, one day, be able to maintain the city's identity as an international financial hub and former British colony.

Glue vaguely remembers a quote by Roland Barthes he once read, stating that language is a kind of legislation and all speech is its code. And perhaps one does not see the power in speech because one sometimes forgets that all speech is a classification. All classifications, by definition, are oppressive. Language—which is a performance of the language system—is neither reactionary nor progressive. It is quite simply fascist. What fascism does is not to prevent speech but to compel speech. Glue makes a mental note to himself—*I will look this quote up later*. But like the quote about snow being white, Glue will forget to look it up, which is good. Because what Barthes said is doubly true for English-language learners.

**THE CONVERSATION** Glue is having with his family about becoming an ESL instructor is reminding Glue of a National Geographic show he watched when he was fifteen. Watching that documentary, Glue began to understand his identity as a Hong Konger. In the show, an Irish man pretends to be a naive tourist in Hong Kong, intentionally letting people scam him. Taxi drivers take longer routes, vendors at street markets raise the prices of the things he's trying to buy. In the episode, a woman asks the foreigner out on a date just to get him to buy things for her. "She was looking for a sugar daddy," he says in the voiceover, his tone serious, no irony whatsoever. "Hong Kong, a free-trade paradise perched on the edge of China, the world's manufacturing powerhouse," the man says. "This might have a reputation of being one of the safest cities in the world, but one thing I know is, wherever you get tourists and cash, you also get scammed." This host speaks like the guy in *Man vs. Wild*. Talk about cities as if they're jungles—that's probably the concept behind the show. "I get scammed so you don't have to," he says, facing the camera.

Glue knows that the news cycle is another example of this. Hong Kong in the eyes of foreigners is a major point of interest, and having the attention of Western media is in itself newsworthy; this is why the National Geographic documentary was aired in Hong Kong and why some Hong Kong–based news outlets reference the fact that the BBC, CNN, or even Fox have covered recent events in Hong Kong—it's like retweeting a retweet of your own tweet.

Glue, who was a teenager in the 2010s in Hong Kong, and having attended international school, is acutely aware that a part of him enjoys assimilating, of being told what to do by popular media. Dutifully, he thought about the Kardashians once in a while throughout the decade. But how, Glue sometimes wonders when he visits his parents in Macau, can this kind of buy-and-redistribute broadcasting model still work after the internet?

Other than some government-produced commercials, and one, or maybe two, afternoon talk shows, everything aired on Macau TV is bought from elsewhere. Glue learned from Po-Wing, who frequents Macau to gamble, that Macau does, however, have distinctive content available on the internet. One example is 微辣 Manner, an independent video production company that produces low-budget local pranks and vlogs—stuff that's purposefully meaningless. The channel became viral with a ten-second clip of a woman ordering ice cream from McDonald's. She's staring at her phone the whole time and grabs the top of the soft serve instead of the cone and walks away. The camera doesn't move. The staff are confused. End of video.[3]

微辣 Manner goes on to partner with a number of established actors and musicians. Eventually, they expand to Southeast Asia and mainland China. But this is what Glue plays on TV when he's drinking beer with Po-Wing—not what his parents watch during dinner.

Commercials continue to play. Glue fixates on the plate of char siu. One of the pieces looks a little undercooked. He eats it.

---

3

**GLUE IS NOT A CBC.** He cannot perform the role of a CBC. Listening to Lester Tse's confident tone and observing his Western-macho mannerisms, Glue recalls an elective course he was enrolled in, back when he was an undergraduate in Toronto. In Design for Business, the instructor discussed the design of subway seats, pointed out that when considering the design of these seats, one needed to take into consideration the passengers. For instance, overworked businesspersons in East Asia, in cities such as Tokyo, Seoul, and Hong Kong, often sleep on the subway on their way to work and, therefore, the design of such seats should be better suited for sleeping. Glue, confused by this remark, asked the instructor why it was the chair that needed to be changed, not the corporate culture, the work-life imbalance. Growing up in Hong Kong, Glue understood that those who work and live in this global financial hub care very little about subway seats; they are much too tired. "Well," noted this professor, "that is precisely why we need to accumulate user feedback." Glue then noted to the professor that subway users in Hong Kong are very unlikely to give feedback. In hypercapitalism, everyone is too preoccupied, trying to squeeze one more second out of each minute. Before Glue could finish, a CBC chimed in. "I don't identify with these stereotypes." The CBC stated, "As an Asian Canadian, I would like to note that it's important we don't generalize. The stereotype that Asians are passive and unlikely to give feedback is simply untrue."

Glue was silent. He did not know the right response. He decided to simply retreat into his seat. Though Glue was incapable of articulating this at the time, the reason why he didn't continue the argument with the CBC was because part of him understood that living in Western society means constantly fighting stereotypes for survival. But by not continuing the discussion, Glue was precisely taking on the stereotype of the passive Asian, unwilling to take action. Both of them, Glue and the CBC, were stuck at an ideological impasse that Canadian state-promoted multiculturalism might not have accounted for. Glue was the stereotypical Asian from Asia—passive, the un-woke international student coming from Confucius's teachings, and perhaps because of his un-wokeness, perceived as a fresh-off-the-boat Chinese—the typical Chinese international student who is ignorant of the norms of the liberal West and says things that are politically incorrect. Glue is precisely the type of person the CBC, who needs to maintain his identity as a CBC, needs to distance himself from. To Glue, the CBC is the typical Westernized Chinese, so preoccupied with performing his "wokeness," his non-Chinese-Chineseness, that denying a discussion that will yield a more nuanced understanding of Asia seems justified. The CBC is not just self-Orientalizing. Glue feels as though this guy is trying to be white. To Glue, the CBC is positioning himself as the Orientalist. Whiteness is at the centre of everything; proximity to it yields freedom. The silence between Glue and the CBC in the classroom affirmed this. "The cause is the consequence," writes Fanon, "you are rich because you are white, you are white because you are rich." The Orientalized, objectified and powerless, becomes a blank screen onto which white fantasies are projected.

**HONG KONG** gears itself towards the white gaze. It's better for business. We all know this. The reason there are red gates and dragon statues and large Chinese characters and red tiles for roofs in Chinatowns around the world is because we need to live in whiteness's fantasies. Back then, residents in Chinatown even hired white architects to build these spaces because we needed to present ourselves as the fantastic imagination of the whites. Or else they'll think that we're taking all their jobs. Once we're done self-Orientalizing for a bit, once we feel safe enough, it's time to be freer, to become whiter.

Now, what are some of the other things we do to become closer to whiteness? Glue can think of a few. But the examples happened post-2019. The filmmaker Chloé Zhao will make a movie about white settlers "being nomadic," which will win her an Oscar, and Andrew Yang will run for president on a campaign based on universal basic income (which Glue thinks will work) and self-Orientalizing, making jokes about being good at math because he's Asian. The two, Zhao and Yang, will do what they need to do to succeed, appealing to whiteness. Some might say that all of this is beautiful, that Hong Kong is a perfect example of East meeting West and that the culture of Hong Kong, so British and so Cantonese at once, is something rare and represents the post-colonial multiculturalism that is possible, where all are happy and coexist after colonization. But people with such beliefs neglect a simple fact: none of this is about collaboration. The British like the word "tolerance": all that is not white is slowly becoming whiter. To think that such things are beautiful, one must be white, or, at the very least, getting close to whiteness.

Despite all of this, Glue's mother seems to like Lester Tse. Maybe because he speaks Mandarin. Or maybe because Gwen seems happy with him. Or maybe because Glue's mom is getting old.

Back to the news: trade wars continue. More people are revealed to have connections to Jeffrey Epstein. Commercial break. Next on the news: more shit is being built in the southern parts of China, around Macau, and yet another Hong Kong politician gets sanctioned by the US. And so on and so on.

Happy Special Administrative Region Establishment Day, everyone.

GWEN IS the one who drives. Glue does not have a licence. Lester, who drove to Macau directly from work, left early to call his business partners in North America. Gwen will be dropping Glue off in Tung Chung, in Lantau Island, not only where Hong Kong International Airport is located but also where the Hong Kong–Zhuhai–Macao Bridge, the world's longest sea-crossing bridge and tunnel system, ends.

At this point in the night, there are no cars, only polluted water lit by the hundreds of yellow lights on the bridge. Glue thinks about all the things that led him to this moment in his life, where his sister, sitting next to him, driving, is trying her best to not engage in conversation with him by focusing all her attention on the road, barely blinking, which makes Glue reluctant to discuss what is on his mind, that it might be best if Gwen slows down a little, that he ate too much barbecue pork at dinner, that his stomach is bloated, that he is starting to feel a little carsick, and though Glue knows that closing his eyes would make him feel a lot better, once he shuts his eyes, in the time between wakefulness and sleep, all he will be thinking about is what he did wrong in his life that led to him having to become an ESL instructor, a job he will despise, at twenty-six years old; everything makes him want to vomit.

Gwen sitting next to Glue, trying to not make conversation, is nothing new. This happened quite often when the two were living together in Toronto. But never has Glue felt uncomfortable next to Gwen.

Right after Gwen Wu completed her MBA at Rotman, she began an internship in Dubai, and, shortly after she completed her internship, she was offered a position as a business consultant in Hong Kong. By then, Glue had dropped out of his MFA in creative writing. So when Glue returned to Hong Kong, he moved in with Gwen. The two of them continued living together, in Tung Chung, at his parents' apartment. Gwen woke up early to commute to work and returned home late. Glue, who preferred working at night, would be in his room, translating PR letters and notices for independent firms and academic institutions. The content varied. Sometimes, he would translate the company's new dress code policy. He would help schools translate a note about updated student norms. "Students are prohibited to use elevators at all times," he wrote. "Technology, though it is a helpful resource for learning, is also a distraction for our students. So access to the following webpages will be blocked from Monday, May 13, 2019."

Occasionally, on the weekends, they would have breakfast together. But Lester Tse moved to Hong Kong and Gwen moved out in May to live with him. With Gwen and Lester's combined income, and help from both their parents, they were able to afford the down payment for an apartment above the Nam Cheong MTR station, giving them access to both the orange subway line that connects them back to Tung Chung and Central, as well as the purple West Rail Line, which connects them to the New Territories. Though geographically close to Sham Shui Po—the poorest and most dense residential area in this special administrative region—their two-bedroom apartment is considered prime real estate. In addition to having a view of the sea from the window in their kitchen, what makes their property more valuable, and a worthy investment, is that it is a mere twelve-minute subway ride from Central, the world's financial hub.

"I didn't know you and Lester were still together." This is what he said when Gwen told Glue she was moving out. Glue knew they were a couple in grad school but wasn't aware that they had continued their relationship. Things stop changing and nothing ever ends.

"He got a job here. One thing led to another and we started seeing each other again. Can you manage on your own?"

But because nothing ever ends, Gwen still sends Glue money each month for the mortgage payments. Glue felt guilty at first, but what he earned as a freelance translator was not enough, so he accepted the money.

Gwen tells Glue to lower his seat and rest. "I'll let you know when we're there." Gwen telling Glue to lower his seat and rest reminds Glue of when they were in Toronto. Glue would be watching Netflix in the living room at night when Gwen returned from the library. At such times, Glue would—and this might be the only time throughout the day Glue expressed caring for his sister directly—tell Gwen that it is late, that she needs to take a shower and get some sleep soon. Glue, now being told what he used to tell Gwen, has no choice but to begin contemplating his past.

**YOUNG GLUE'S** ability to read score was so slow, his timing so imprecise, plus the fact that land and, by extension, living space in Hong Kong is worth more than anything else, the acoustics of their Tung Chung apartment, where they grew up, where the piano is next to the dinner table, next to the couch, in front of the TV (which is almost always on), in between two bookshelves because it is important to maximize the use of every inch of space in the city of Hong Kong, there is, behind the piano, between the couch and the dinner table (and Glue does not know why they have one), a small red trampoline, Glue's playing of Chopin's Piano Concerto no. 1 is mixed with the sound of the washing of dishes and the flushing of the toilet and the radio in Gwen's bedroom as well as everything else that is happening in Hong Kong in the early 2010s: the Umbrella Revolution, the annual July 1 protests, the perpetual rising of housing prices, the fact that it is becoming more expensive to sit in a café just to be away, albeit momentarily, from one's crowded apartment, more expensive to take a taxi, to take the MTR, to take the bus, to take the minibus, to eat, to drink water, and to breathe in Asia's global financial hub where more and more primary, secondary, and post-secondary students and faculty are committing suicide every year, children are still, despite all of this, trying to learn how to play the piano, and here, everything that comes from every piano played by a child in every house-hold's crowded apartment sounds like diarrhea.

*THOUGH GLUE'S* playing of the piano sounded like watery shit, he could run. Glue represented his public school in competitions as a long-distance runner, and even won some awards. His parents didn't care, though. Desperate for their son to be proficient with a European classical instrument, and because they were certain that Glue would fail the state's standardized tests required for all public school students in Hong Kong, they transferred Glue to the Queen's Music Academy in Diamond Hill. Their plan was that Glue, after having received an international school education, would be prepared to apply for post-secondary institutions overseas. Glue, from the ages of fourteen to seventeen, commuted for an hour and a half from Tung Chung to this school. Glue would take the Tung Chung Line to Lai King, transfer onto the red line to Yau Ma Tei, and transfer to the green line to get to Diamond Hill station, and, there, at the Hollywood Plaza's bus terminal, he would board a green minivan to get to the top of Diamond Hill, where the Queen's Music Academy, with its European architecture—the Jehovahjireh Concert Hall and its parking lot that looked like a Roman battle arena, all of which were designed by Chinese acousticians and architects—sat proudly next to three other public schools with less funding.

Glue's new school was also right next to the Diamond Hill Funeral Parlour. During classes, Glue could see, outside the window of the classrooms of this private institution, smoke rising into the sky from the funeral home, black vans pulling up with sympathy flowers on top. The flowers were white, light green, and purple. Mourners stood on the streets, waiting. He could smell the smoke—the burning of dead bodies—when he ran laps around the basketball court during gym class. All the while, above all the students, on the top of this ten-storey-high school, stood a bright iron cross. At night, the cross was lit up by white lights. There was also a penthouse, where the principal resided.

Glue never met the principal. But he often heard things about him. The principal's given name, 丁永恒, literally translated to "eternity." The man's name sounded as if it were taken directly from a Chinese translation of the Bible. Mr. Ding Wing Hang had connections with government officials. He established scholarships and gave the money to the children of these officials—large bribes that their children accepted on their parents' behalf. With this system in place, Mr. Ding continued developing his own property on top of this Occidentalized school.

But none of this matters. After transferring here, Glue gave up on playing the piano and began spitting notes into a horn. It was time to further Glue's assimilation. What better way to show you're down to assimilate than by joining the orchestra. The French horn is an instrument that requires strong tongue movements but very little fingering, and the scores were also simpler to Glue.

Glue's eyes are closed. Sitting in Gwen's car, with his seat reclined, this twenty-six-year-old Glue starts moving his tongue inside his mouth, imagining that he is playing the French horn, articulating, in a fast and controlled manner, each of the notes of the scale by tonguing. (Imagine softly closing your lips and spitting using only your tongue.) The higher notes require a more aggressive attack. He spits into the air and his saliva lands on his own forehead and he wipes it off with the inside of his elbow. Gwen tells him to stop doing whatever he's doing.

"You're disgusting," Gwen says quietly, not so much to Glue, Glue thinks, but to remind herself that her brother is disgusting.

The two do not talk for the rest of the ride.

THE QUEEN'S Music Academy, an Occidentalized Roman Empire in post-colonial Hong Kong, had but one French horn player in the orchestra. So naturally Glue, though he hardly knew how to play, joined as the second French horn. Glue sat amongst other students who were the best at their respective instruments. Glue also joined mid-semester and only knew Jeremy, who'd transferred to the school at the same time as Glue. Jeremy was the precise opposite of Glue, a child prodigy and the concertmaster at his previous school. Here, he never showed up to rehearsals, yet the spotlight was always on him during performances. Jeremy also excelled academically, of course, and would later attend Juilliard for graduate studies and then Yale to receive a second master's in musical arts. Everyone knew Glue as, not Glue, but Jeremy's friend, the runner, the jock who'd transferred in at the same time.

"Glue, fuck it. This orchestra isn't going to make it anywhere," Jeremy said. "We put on a pathetic show at the end of the year to tell these wealthy parents who don't give two fucks about music that their kids aren't doing nothing. Just pretend you're playing. I bet the conductor won't even give two shits."

For the entire semester, Glue simply moved his fingers without blowing much air into his instrument. The conductor glanced at Glue.

"Alright. Let's just hear from the brass section." The conductor wore silver-framed glasses. He sported a goatee, and his hairstyle, with the sides buzzed and the rest of his hair short and spiky, reminded Glue of American teenagers from nineties movies. Jeremy told Glue that he often saw the conductor driving students home in his car—the girls looked as young as fourteen. The conductor drove a cabriolet. If one happened upon this guy on the street, with his tight black shirt and too much product in his hair, one would be inclined to think that he was a director of pornographic films, not a teacher of classical music.

"Something sounds off," said the (alleged) pedophile with a goatee. "Let's just hear from the horns."

The other horn player—two years Glue's senior—had played the instrument for over five years, and when Glue missed a note, she would shoot a sharp glance in his direction. *Why are you even here?* the look seemed to say. Glue, years later, will receive the same look at a bar, in Toronto, when a white man, drunk, will push Glue aside in a narrow hallway leading to the washroom. The man will glance back at Glue. *Why are you even here?* It's a sharp glance.

Nothing ever changes. The man's glance will remind Glue of his days in the orchestra—the beginning of his assimilation. Because of all of this, Glue is now ready to become an ESL instructor.

Glue will soon realize that, all his life, he's always felt trapped.

"You're a runner, Glen Wu," said the porn-director conductor. "You should have better control of your breathing than that."

**NOT WANTING** to embarrass himself any longer, for every song that the orchestra played, Glue asked Jeremy to find him the third French horn's score to play instead. As the third French horn, Glue, on average, had only to play one or maybe two notes each bar. All he did was hold the notes while the first French horn played the melody. No one noticed that Glue was not playing the tune of the second horn. Or maybe the conductor simply gave up on Glue.

Being part of the orchestra had nothing to do with music. It was, to Glue, a chore—structured and repetitive—like going for afternoon tea and eating crumpets—chores that are routinely performed by middle to upper-middle-class Hong Kongers to become closer to whiteness. Playing for the orchestra was nothing more than a routine activity in this post-colonial place, where the cause is the consequence, where rich people want to differentiate themselves from the locals, and private institutions like these need to separate themselves from the public schools that surround them in order to attract parents who want their children to be more Westernized.

This is natural because "the colonial world is a Manichean world. It is not enough for the settler to delimit physically, that is to say with the help of the army and the police force, the place of the native. As if to show the totalitarian character of colonial exploitation the settler paints the native as a sort of quintessence of evil" (Frantz Fanon, *The Wretched of the Earth*).

In his school uniform, a tight cotton white shirt with purple stripes and a purple tie, Glue, three times a week, blew air repeatedly into this brass instrument he knew little about. He sometimes imagined himself as an animal, being held captive in a zoo. What kind of animal would Glue be? A giraffe? No, Glue was skinny and tall but his neck was not that long. His classmates were right—a camel would be a better fit. Glue, though many did not notice this because he wore glasses back then, had sleepy eyes—a result of masturbating himself to sleep at night and then needing to commute an hour and a half to get to school every morning. The same camel face would follow Glue to his first job, at Disneyland.

Glue missed another note. The first French horn served him yet another chilling look.

"I have a similar story," Elle told Glue. This was at a bar, years later, when Glue was an undergrad in Canada. "I once performed in a public speaking competition. And I was the Queen!"

Glue looked at Elle, confused. The two had met at the Design for Business class at the University of Toronto. Elle reached out to Glue after the incident with the CBC and the two of them, though they were not able to articulate their frustrations with the exchange until later, met for coffee, and together, they took out their phones and dropped out of the class.

"Before I came here, I was at this really bureaucratic school in Singapore," Elle said. "And there were these public speaking competitions, where we were all asked to show off our English to the whites. I had a kind of British accent, 'cause my English tutor was British. So anyways. I decided that I'd perform the Queen's twenty-first-birthday speech."

"Using her accent?" Glue asked.

"Of course! I won, too! My impression was so good. So, because I was so good, I had to perform at the end-of-year ceremony. I was fourteen back then. I was down to try anything and thought, why not? But the teachers didn't tell me that in the audience were these members from the British embassy. When the lights turned on, I saw them in the front row. Just a row of blond heads and confused faces. Like, why is this Chinese girl telling us that she's declaring that *her whole life whether it be long or short shall be devoted to your service and the service of our great imperial family to which we all belong?*" Elle said this with pride. Glue laughed.

Elle dressed well, Glue always thought. She enjoyed searching for vintage goods in luxury brands. The watch she was wearing that day, Glue remembers, was something his late grandmother, who spent her entire life in Hong Kong, would have worn, the ones by one of those Swiss brands that were around since the 1800s (Jaeger-LeCoultre?), a small rectangle with thick black numbers and diamonds encrusted on the edges. Elle's skin was soft and white and when Glue looked at that watch and its red leather strap, Glue's idea of "old" and "new" began to blend. Glue remembers staring at Elle's watch when she did an impression of the Queen. Glue remembers feeling as though the meaning of history can always change.

"**DON'T WORRY,** man. You'll be fine. Your family's got connections and you go to a good school and all. I'm sure you'll figure it out." Po-Wing, back then, was a second-year student at the University of Hong Kong, studying physiology. When Glue moved to Toronto, he and Po-Wing sometimes called each other on WhatsApp. Po-Wing was interested in Glue's life in Toronto, but he never talked about his life in Hong Kong. "What's there to talk about? I commute there once in a while, write a test, come back, that's pretty much it."

Nothing ever changes. When Gwen drops Glue off, Glue texts Po-Wing, asking him if he wants to grab a beer. The two of them still meet outside the same 7-Eleven across from the Tung Chung Post Office. Glue and Po-Wing, just as they did when they were teenagers, spend this evening playing basketball together at the courts in Tung Chung. Covered in sweat, the two visit the 7-Eleven for a late-night snack—fish balls that taste so artificial they crumble into dust once they touch your teeth. Glue puts one in his mouth.

"I like that the beer is cheap here and you can drink wherever." Glue washes the dusty fish ball down with some beer, which makes his stomach growl. Being constipated reminds Glue that his body is no longer young. His metabolism is slowing down. His health is certain to deteriorate more rapidly if he keeps bingeing alcohol. But living alone, and deciding to become an ESL instructor, something he's long dreaded, Glue feels that, at any given time, he might easily fall back into a drunken stupor, reverting back to his post-Disney state, wandering, four years later, inebriated, on the same streets at night.

**THE NEXT** day, Glue wakes up at noon. He sits on the toilet. Glue, whenever he picks up his phone, expects to see messages from May and Elle. There are no messages from them. Browsing through his phone, Glue comes across an ad: the Ontario Institute for Studies in Education has a sale running on online programs. This is no coincidence: last night Glue's mother texted him the letters *IELTS* and *ESL*. After ignoring the first two ads, Glue succumbs to the algorithm upon seeing a discount. "In the colonies the economic infrastructure is also a superstructure. The cause is the consequence. . . . The intellectual sheds all that calculating, all those strange silences, those ulterior motives that devious thinking and secrecy as he gradually plunges deeper among the people" (Frantz Fanon, *The Wretched of the Earth*).

Glue ends up signing up for a TEFL (Teaching English as a Foreign Language) certificate, which costs CAN$1,170.68; this is after a 20 percent discount. The discount code is

BLCKFRIDAYSALE. Why is there a Black Friday sale in July? It doesn't matter. The discount code works. Glue decides to get a TEFL certificate because the alternative, a CELTA (Certificate in Teaching English to Speakers of Other Languages), costs way more—$2,495.56; this is probably because the CELTA is administered by Cambridge University. The CELTA is also more widely recognized, especially in former British colonies. How far are you willing to go to assimilate? the system asks. Not that far, Glue answers.

Glue pays the money. And Glue's parents, who paid the down payment for this apartment, upon learning that Glue has finally enrolled to become an ESL instructor, are overjoyed.

So here he is. This twenty-six-year-old Glue might finally be earning a stable living. Finally, he will fulfil his destiny and become an ESL teacher who teaches English to the people in this post-colonial place. He will be contributing to society by maintaining Hong Kong's identity as a former colony and now financial hub. The future of this city—its youth—depends on Glue now.

But Glue is still constipated because "instead of being the coordinated crystallization of the people's innermost aspirations, instead of being the most tangible, immediate product of popular mobilization, national consciousness is nothing but a crude, empty, fragile shell" (Frantz Fanon, *The Wretched of the Earth*).

The next morning, Glue wakes up feeling extremely

hungry and heads to the wet market downstairs for some steamed buns. Standing in line are cabin attendants, waiting to get a decent breakfast before departing the city.

**GLUE DOESN'T** mind waking up late in the afternoon one day and before the sun rises the next. An irregular schedule, not living in structured time, waking up when his body wakes up and sleeping when he's tired, fits Glue best. Mechanical repetitiveness is what Glue always wanted to avoid. Elle, to an extent, was the same. Elle enrolled in a fashion program at Toronto Metropolitan University while Glue was at teachers' college, thinking that having a full-time job, a safe and stable career as a teacher, was what he wanted. But shortly after he graduated from teachers' college, he soon realized that he did not want to start a full-time teaching position. It would be too repetitive. He was young. The mere thought of routine work reminded Glue of playing the French horn, holding long notes, for hours, as those around him played the melody. To this day, Glue becomes nervous whenever classical music plays. After rehearsals, to unwind on his commute home, Glue would flood his ears with sad Cantopop songs on his green iPod

Mini. When it became too depressing, he would turn the music off but leave his headphones on and play Snake on his Nokia flip phone. After he left the orchestra, he stopped listening to music altogether. Hearing music, especially classical music, still makes him fear that all his thoughts will contract into a single cell and that one cell will be eaten by a gorilla.

Glue's own past, to him, feels foreign. He never questioned his parents' decision to enrol him in a random music school an hour and a half away from where he lived, which is good, because now, having lived in Canada for eight years and having then returned to Hong Kong, Glue finds that everything that was once familiar feels detached, which is also good. Becoming indifferent to the past—that is the mentality one needs to have in order to continue living in this post-colonial place.

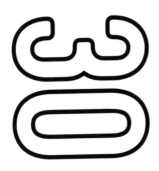

**INSTEAD OF** beginning his teaching career, Glue enrolled in a graduate program in creative writing, which led to Glue's parents supporting Glue a little less, giving him just enough money each month for groceries. So, in graduate school and in need of money, Glue took on a part-time instructor position at Atlantia Education's after-school program. He learned from getting fired from Disneyland that he needed to suck it up. The cause is the consequence and money is freedom. Earn some money; that is how you can become free.

Atlantia is a private institution in North York, a one-hour-and-fifteen-minute commute from where Glue lived in downtown Toronto. On the weekends, Glue would take the subway from Wellesley station to North York and transfer to a bus which took him to a bus terminal, where he would transfer to another bus and then walk for another ten minutes to arrive at the campus.

Glue's students at Atlantia were mostly children of Chinese immigrants or first-generation Chinese Canadians.

This didn't surprise Glue. The students' parents were raised in the rigorous test-based education system of East Asia and found Canada's slightly more relaxed form of education to be lazy. Bullshit schools like Atlantia Education leverage the model minority myth. More is more. The school didn't even try to hide this. Glue had been raised to buy into the idea of a cram school. But a cram school, the sole purpose of which is to add additional classes outside of day-school hours so that students will "perform better" academically, is counterproductive, Glue knew; such establishments only serve to highlight test-based education's oppressiveness. It's denial of growth. It's love of death. It's necrophilia.

*We all self-Orientalize.* Glue remembers thinking this when he found out the school he was working for was established by Chinese entrepreneurs. Glue, in just a few years, will also take advantage of his own stereotypes. Nothing about his identity is about him, Glue will soon realize. He will also understand that all of this is carefully designed. In capitalism, minorities take advantage of other minorities' disadvantages. Glue will tell himself that he needs to do this to survive, to make a little more money before he stops. But when one takes advantage of self-Orientalizing to survive, and one works in education and educates the youth while self-Orientalizing to appeal to Confucian-capitalist values, one ends up with, not private institutions and Occidentalized Roman Empires as campuses, which would be too crass, and those tend to exist in the colonial worlds away from the West, but a result that is more or less the same.

Atlantia's campus, located in North York, consists of portables. Each portable contains a number of classrooms that are filled with worn-out wooden chairs and desks. It looks shabby. But perhaps its shabbiness is intentional. *This is a place for studying the old-fashioned way*, the place says. Seeing this place, Glue was reminded of his parents. If he had grown up in Canada, his parents would likely have found Atlantia's look, its ugliness, its longing-for-the-past aesthetic, attractive. *None of that fancy neoliberal bullshit*, they would think—a somewhat radical yet regressive way of thinking about education that somehow simultaneously rejects and reinforces capitalist values.

GLUE, before he started working at Atlantia Education, read that the school was praised for its diverse syllabus. For its Grade 10 English class, students read *Othello*, *The Joy Luck Club*, and *The Martian*.

"Mr. Wu, I have a question, if you don't mind. I want to know if this book was written for white people." Glue's student was asking about Amy Tan's *The Joy Luck Club*.

Glue paused. He looked at his copy of *The Joy Luck Club*, its blue cover and red font, two golden dragons breathing out white clouds that curled inwards on either side of the book's title. It was as though the designer saw a menu from a random Chinese restaurant in the West and placed it on the book. "Yes," Glue said, a slight tone of regret in his voice. "Most things written in English, especially back then, had a white audience in mind. Nonetheless, *The Joy Luck Club* is an important piece of Asian American literature that we need to read."

Glue could not blame Amy Tan. Self-Orientalizing,

appealing to the public's imagination of the Orient, yields book sales.

"An important piece of Asian American literature written for white people?" The teenagers were not convinced.

"It is important to share our history with others," Glue said. These students, all of whom were fifteen, were probably better informed than whoever designed the curriculum.

"Isn't that for history class, Mr. Wu?" another asserted.

Glue took a deep breath. "Well—"

"We only talk about the world wars in history class," another student said.

"Yes," said Glue. "Many topics, especially those about our history, aren't actually covered in history classes, which is why we need literature."

"Then why don't we combine history class and literature class, Mr. Wu?"

"We should probably do that, Sophie." Glue decided to stop defending this education system.

"I think we can combine literature with science classes, too," said another.

"Another great suggestion, Emily. That's a fantastic idea."

"Then why aren't we doing that, Mr. Wu?"

"I'm liking all of these ideas and where this conversation is going. Let's continue to think about it. We should return to this conversation later. Let's read some *Joy Luck Club* first. Perhaps we'll be able to have a more nuanced discussion afterwards."

*The Joy Luck Club* is a novel about how having a Chinese upbringing fucks your life up in America. Though the book might be a little bit more complex than that, this was Glue's initial thought upon finishing it. Glue read *The Joy Luck Club* for English class when he himself was in high school, in Hong Kong. Ten years later, in Canada, he was teaching it. This was to be expected. After all, "the unpreparedness of the educated classes, the lack of practical links between them and the mass of the people, their laziness, and, let it be said, their cowardice at the decisive moment of the struggle will give rise to tragic mishaps" (Frantz Fanon, *The Wretched of the Earth*). One tragic mishap being that Glue will become an ESL instructor.

He became popular with his students. Being the good person in a bad situation was much too easy. Glue let the students discuss *The Joy Luck Club* amongst themselves and did not make the completion of in-class worksheets compulsory. This was enough to earn the students' affection.

**GLUE**, who grew up with a learning disability, had struggled with focusing. Retaining information from written texts seemed impossible to him throughout his secondary school years. But that changed. In addition to reading works by French philosophers in undergrad, Glue read works by bell hooks and Paulo Freire, radical thinkers that challenged top-down education. The reason he did not succeed in secondary school was not because of his learning disability, he realized, but because of Hong Kong's rigidly structured test-based education system.

What Glue was doing at Atlantia Education was merely reaffirming the system. Glue was making the students feel freer so the system could continue to oppress them. This made him feel powerful. It made him feel Western. It made him feel white. Western countries interfere in world conflicts. And when they do that, Glue thinks, they smell like heroes, here in the name of freedom to liberate everything. In reality, their end game is simply to orient (and sometimes reorient) power towards themselves. Everybody knows this. When the French left Vietnam, the Americans entered. For the same reason, the Americans involved themselves in the Korean War. They established military bases in Japan, made it their neo-colony. They position themselves as China watchers, the world's police. But there are some who don't see this as a problem.

A microcosm of this exists on a societal level as well; it is far too easy for white men to receive praise for moderately good deeds. Glue recalled watching a clip of a government official from San Francisco receiving thunderous applause for accepting a "comfort women" statue. Of course, the US itself was complicit in the rise of right-wing nationalism in Japan, which, eventually, led to the country denying many of its war crimes. All of this shaped the public's imagination. And led to people of Japanese descent, in San Francisco, denying that the comfort women were sex slaves.

Good thing Glue studied acting, because he was fully aware that his being lenient on his students' completion of in-class work wasn't changing a thing. In fact, like fair-trade coffee, recycling, the Green New Deal (to some extent), as well as corporate feminism and self-care, what Glue was doing was nothing more than feel-good ideology, gentle gestures that make a dire situation seem bearable; he was changing the design of the seats on subways instead of changing the system. He was delaying people's realization of the necessity of progress and radical change. He was denying growth. He was being necrophilous. "The necrophilous person is driven by the desire to transform the organic into the inorganic," writes Erich Fromm, "to approach life mechanically, as if all living persons were things. . . . Memory, rather than experience—having, rather than being—is what counts. . . . He loves control, and in the act of controlling he kills life."

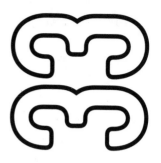

**WHILE GLUE** was teaching at Atlantia, he started remembering the days he was a student at the Queen's Music Academy, listening to his teacher's lesson while, across the street, smoke rose from the Diamond Hill Funeral Parlour.

ON SUNDAYS, after a full day of teaching, Glue, a graduate school student who had creative writing class the next day, would spend the evening drinking. As he did when he worked for Disney, he drank cheap whiskey, which burned his throat and gave him heavy hangovers. Glue would miss creative writing class. He would miss his deadlines as well. He also couldn't write. He spent most of his waking mornings hungover, watching videos on YouTube.

Late one afternoon, two years or so after they began dating, Elle walked into Glue's apartment. Gwen was working at the library that day. Glue was alone, kneeling in front of the toilet. He had just puked. Elle looked at him and shut the door.

Glue remembered lying in bed. He felt as though his mind was floating in the middle of a dark sea between wakefulness and sleep. He stared at the ceiling and saw lights reflected from the apartments across the street, shapes and forms morphing and disintegrating into nothingness. He tried to breathe through his mouth. His breath, for some reason, felt clean. When he turned his head, he saw Elle lying next to him.

"I like your eyes," Elle said.

Glue recalled watching a clip on TikTok. A basketball coach decided to take a player out of the game after committing a mistake. The coach did not scold the player, simply asked him to take a breather. But Glue could tell, from looking at this player's face, that he knew he had messed up. The coach put the player in again minutes later and the player performed well. This made Glue smile.

# GENESIS

# HAS

# NOTHING

≡

# TO DO

# WITH GOD

**MAY**, the person Glue started seeing after he returned to Hong Kong, has not been responding to Glue's messages. Glue has sent four messages but May has not responded. If May will not answer, Glue will compose a reply from May instead. *Hey Glue* (typing out your own name feels funny). *I'll be away for a bit. I wanted to tell you when we met but you looked exhausted. I'm travelling now. I'm in Yangshuo. The mountains are beautiful here. I'm at a Starbucks. The Starbucks here looks exactly the same as the one in Tung Chung next to the MTR station. I'll be in touch when I'm back. Sorry, again, for not telling you before I left.*

Glue doesn't really think May is in Yangshuo. Glue just remembers seeing images on Instagram taken by Asian American influencers visiting Yangshuo. He saw the mountains and water and the influencers with their tanned skin, decked out in athletic wear from head to toe (#Aloyoga), reminding him of May who, whenever they go out in Tung Chung, wears only athletic wear.

Glue is still constipated. He decides to eat dim sum. After filling his stomach with siu mai and barbecue pork buns, Glue decides that he needs some fruit to deal with his indigestion. Perhaps doing some cardio will help. He visits one of the local courts for a game of pickup basketball. Glue enjoys playing basketball whenever he has the chance, but he's not good anymore and his back aches. High school kids kick his ass. This did not bother Glue at first, when he began to play pickup basketball when he returned to Hong Kong, but now, and perhaps this has to do with him being constipated, twice, in the same evening, he gets into fights with high school kids over their petty foul calls. Perhaps he's just upset that May is not replying to him. But the main reason Glue is angry on the court is because last night he started his TEFL training. In TEFL, everything is test-based. There is no room for interpretation or discussions. Absolute answers only. To pass the course, Glue answered multiple-choice questions about grammar. He learned nothing about what it is like to acquire a new language.

Glue recalls a clip from the Ali G show[4] where Ali G,

4

who was interviewing Chomsky, asks why we don't create a new language.

"Instead of like the word 'bread,' you have something like . . . methalob, or, or meth-la, or, no no no, or . . . latheeena."

Chomsky explains to Ali G that no one would pay the slightest attention to a new language. Chomsky's voice was stoic, devoid of judgment.

"But you could earn a lot of money, if—"

"It's a waste of time."

Rather than making him laugh, rewatching this clip made Glue sad. His Chinese is imperfect now, because he has not used it since he left for Canada at the age of eighteen. He can't read simplified characters and cannot write traditional Chinese using any input system other than Pinyin, which requires nothing more than to use the English alphabet to simulate the sound of Chinese characters.

Glue is an ESL student. No language belongs to Glue. But poetry undermines linguistics. Though Glue can't articulate this, it was one of the main reasons why, at a certain point in time, he wanted to write.

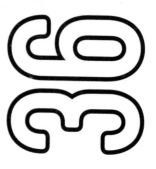

THE HEAT AND HUMIDITY has drained Glue's ability to comprehend time. Glue has, however, achieved a state of mind that allows him to work on the modules that allow him to acquire a licence to teach ESL. He has also created a daily routine for himself that requires him to apply to at least two ESL positions a day. He will not have lunch until he finishes the application for one job and will not have dinner until he has applied for a second job. Throughout August, Glue's desire to write returns to him. He finds these notes on his phone:

🍲 The cow intestines boil in the pot, in front of the old man who is selling cow intestine soup at the wet market, and he looks as though he understands the innards' nature and takes joy in serving his understanding to those who share the same understanding.

🚇 Air conditioning makes the subway cold. Passengers, sweaty, with sunscreen all over their bodies, need to put

on their windbreakers that are tied around their waists
so as not to catch a cold. The stickiness of their skin
makes it difficult for them to put on their windbreakers
easily. This must be what it feels like to be a sausage.
(This is especially true for passengers boarding the
MTR at Sunny Bay station, where they have just spent
a full day at Disneyland.)

※ For as long as we've had outlet malls, we've had
suburbs. For as long as we've had suburbs, we've had
airports. For as long as we've had airports, we've had
duty-free stores that sell luxury skincare products and
whiskey. Purchasing discounted goods for friends is a
way for suburban residents to sustain relationships with
their peers who live in the city.

But none of what Glue writes on his phone inspires him
to write more.

Glue, again, imagines May writing to him.

*I just felt like I really needed to tell you I took something of
yours without you knowing. I should also tell you that I haven't
stolen anything like that in the last ten years. I don't know
why, I felt like a child again and I just took something of yours
when you weren't aware.*

After writing this, Glue wonders for a second if "May"
is actually May's real name.

Glue always deletes these messages to May that he
writes to himself.

**THE SCREEN** in front of Glue's treadmill has the word "live" in the top right-hand corner. Central, though only twenty-odd minutes away by MTR, feels distant through the screen. Protestors are occupying one of Central's main streets. Protestors are also occupying the Hong Kong International Airport. But Tung Chung, ten minutes away from the airport, for now, is perfectly quiet this Sunday afternoon.

Still unable to shit, Glue goes through everything in his two-bedroom apartment once more. Something of his has been stolen. There are very few things left in the apartment. Gwen, whose refined taste far exceeds that of Glue's, bought all the furniture in their apartment. Glue urged his sister to take the furniture with her when she moved, but she refused. She told Glue to keep it—she'd considered the lighting of the living room and selected the furniture to match the space. Glue wonders if this is true. Gwen furnished the apartment much like how she furnished the one they shared in Canada.

Glue has seldom entered his sister's room. They respected each other's privacy and knew that, when one of them was in the mood to talk, they would hang out in the living space.

The wooden floor is dusty. There is no bed, only an old mattress that she and Glue should have thrown out months before.

Glue is still constipated. Unable to sleep, he decides to take a walk.

The MTR station downstairs is destroyed. Police officers, in all-black riot gear, are patrolling the scene. No protestors. The entrance gates are broken, glass is scattered all over the ground, and the ticket machines are smashed to shambles. Glue starts walking away from the station, through the pedestrian tunnels and underground biking lanes, all the way to the riverside, where the Ngong Ping 360 gondola lifts that take tourists to the Tian Tan Buddha during the day hang above the river. Staring at the lifts that hang above his head, Glue no longer feels he's in Tung Chung but inside a larger organism—that all of the stillness that surrounds him is part of a system giving mobility to something larger. But what that thing is, he cannot tell. His stomach growls.

"I stole something from you," May said.

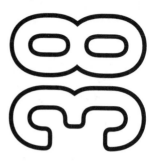

**WHEN A PERSON IS BORN**, the brain starts comprehending the world by telling itself stories. The adult brain will sometimes convert to religion because, to the brain, religion works the same way childhood memories do. Take Christianity, for example. The opening book of the Bible, Genesis, tells a story that explains how the world came to be, using, not logic, but narratives derived from a number of religions in the same geographic area that reinforce a set of ideologies. Since narratives in religious texts are stories used to promote a set of ideas, for those who are raised Christian, narratives in the Bible become a set of principles through which to interpret the world. But the human brain is frail, and even for those who are not religious, at least sometimes in adulthood it becomes so tired that it wants to reboot, returning briefly to the point of its childhood memories, its basic principles. At these moments, religions and cults alike hack in. For the same reason, conspiracy theories appeal to those who cannot comprehend the unfairness of capitalism.

Running will disrupt the workings of this larger thing.

Glue runs along the riverbank, passes by an Indian restaurant near the pier. His stomach is bloated. His back is sweaty. But breathing becomes easier as he runs. Glue runs around a large square surrounded by white concrete private apartment buildings with green window frames. In the centre of the empty square is an open area where children play during the day. He runs around the circle, passing each shop four times, a 7-Eleven, a small drugstore, a German restaurant, a supermarket, a Thai restaurant, a kindergarten, and a hair salon, before deciding to enter the park next to the Tung Chung Novotel. He runs past a pagoda where the elderly practise tai chi in the morning. He doesn't stop. Lights in the buildings that surround him start to turn on. Thousands of eyes from the windows might be watching him as he sprints through the park, but he doesn't care. *So what? Let them watch*. He starts racing towards the airport.

*It's as if a shrimp appeared in my heart*, May said to Glue. Why is this bothering him? Running while thinking about this makes everything around Glue become unfamiliar. Reality's interface flashes across Glue's vision, quickly refreshing, congealing into a set of fundamental principles, before expanding and re-becoming the reality he is familiar with.

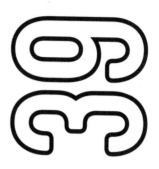

**HE RETURNS** home and shits.

The next day, Glue wakes up hungry. He hears the beeping of Octopus cards on his way to the wet market. The MTR station—destroyed the night before—is now in perfect condition. People with suitcases in hand and purses on their shoulders are leaving Tung Chung for Central to go to work. The ticket machines that were smashed to pieces just last night are now fully functional.

Last night, an event that belonged to another time, another space, for a moment, randomly inserted itself into Glue's present.

*IT IS* the beginning of September. May is back. May feels much better. "I feel much better," May says. "It's important to be away for a bit." May hugs Glue, asks what he has been up to.

Glue does not tell May that he is applying to become an ESL teacher. May, sensing that Glue probably does not want to talk about work, tells Glue that she stayed in a small hostel in the mountains somewhere north of Taipei and shows him pictures of the tea houses she visited during the day.

"I worked here during the day," May says. "It's quite nice, isn't it."

*It's quite nice isn't it.* This phrase strikes Glue as oppressively British. There is also something about people who just returned from vacations, something about their tone, that bothers Glue. Why that is, he has no idea.

"I feel so much better after being away for some time," says May.

But Glue wants to talk to May. He isn't so much annoyed at May but annoyed by the fact that he can be so easily annoyed. May is feeling better. He should be happy for her. He is happy for her.

"Why Taipei?" Glue asks.

"Ask something else," says May. When they started sleeping together, they agreed on two rules. The second one is that they don't have to answer questions they don't want to. Perhaps the rules to their relationship still stand, will always stand between them.

Looking at the images May is showing him, of the terraces of tea houses in the mountains and bamboo chairs, Glue, all of a sudden, feels writerly. He asks May a writerly question: If there were a machine that could simulate reality to a point where one could perceive and understand everything as reality itself, would she enter it? After a moment of silence, May tells him that yes, she would, but only if one thing about the world might be changed. What that one thing is, she says she will tell him later.

"Let's go back to yours," May says simply.

It happens to Glue sometimes. Sometimes, when he feels annoyed at himself, he is motivated to try to think creatively. Is creativity something that Glue uses to disguise his flaws? Glue decides to not think about this.

May has handcuffs with her this time. She takes out the orange butt plug Glue hides under his bed.

"How did you know that was there?"

May rubs lubricant on the butt plug and starts fingering

Glue's anus, and in one swift movement inserts the butt plug. Glue squeals. But despite his having felt a sudden shot of pleasure, Glue's penis remains flaccid, which has never happened to him before.

"Are you okay?" May asks.

"I'm sorry," Glue says.

"Is something bothering you?"

"I don't know."

"You're not thinking about what I stole, right? If that's the case, you don't need to worry about it. I promise you that whatever it is, it's not something you really need to have."

Glue thinks that it's probably something that never belonged to him in the first place. All he can think about right now, lying face down on his pillow, with the butt plug still up his ass, is the Tung Chung MTR station that was completely destroyed, and of the police, in riot gear, patrolling the scene. The same station was fully fixed and functional the morning after. He tries to stop thinking about the station, but Tian Tan Buddha sits above him, watching, in the mountains above. He thinks about the image of the Guanyin, pointing at him and Po-Wing. Tung Chung is making sure that these two things, and not anything else, are all Glue can think about at this moment.

"Don't be sorry," May says. She pulls out the butt plug and tosses it on the floor. For a while, they lie there in silence.

"Sometimes I think that the purpose of life," May says, "is to either create or destroy, nothing more. I wouldn't think that if I lived in a completely secular world. If that isn't possible, I'd want to make sure that at the very least, Christianity wouldn't exist, or at least that no one is allowed to raise their children religious." May sighs. "I think raising your child religious is a form of child abuse. Why are we allowed to pressure an immature mind to live in line with a set of beliefs without consent? It's so fascist. I really hate that an entire belief system can be imposed on a young mind. I think that as parents, there's already so much that you're doing to shape the lives of your children. They should at least have the freedom to choose to believe or not believe in something."

May is becoming philosophical as well. Writerliness is contagious, Glue concludes.

May opens the blinds next to the bed. In some of the apartments nearby, people are watching TV. Lights from their screens flicker.

"If I continue living in this world," May continues, "my existence will be reliant on me being in opposition to the things I hate. It's tiring."

The MTR station downstairs with its red-and-white logo shines brightly through the window, into the bedroom, and onto the ceiling.

"Let's not consider it a religion," Glue says.

"What do you mean?"

Glue is feeling writerly, he might even be feeling like an intellectual, a feeling he seldom feels and will feel less often after he begins to fully assimilate into his role as an ESL teacher. "I learned this from listening to some podcast a while back. Genesis has nothing to do with a God. It is just a description of a childhood memory, a detailed account of a mind trying to understand and comprehend components the world is made up of, things like light and darkness, sky and ground, the names of plants and animals, and so on. It has nothing to do with the creation of the earth. It's a description of a learning curve, structures that a mind is inventing to make sense of how things in the world work."

What is the point of saying such a thing, May's face seems to say. These are probably the words going through May's mind. But May doesn't say anything. Perhaps she doesn't want to shit on Glue's parade. Glue feels vulnerable now, which, he knows, will make him become more and more attracted to May. Glue is at risk of falling in love.

The orange butt plug sits next to the window. Lights from television screens of apartments nearby continue to shine through, giving light to this compartmentalized world.

A plane takes off.

# GLUE

# AND

四

DESTROY

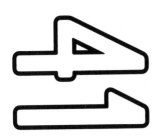

GLUE IS over at Po-Wing's watching *Godzilla vs. Kong*. The film has yet to be released in cinemas but Po-Wing, somehow, has access to an unreleased edit of the movie on a thumb drive that he says he needs to return right after the viewing. "We need to watch this shit before they hand it over to the censors," he says.

A giant Japanese lizard punching a giant American monkey with a side of Sapporo, and weed is what suits this twenty-six-year-old soon-to-be ESL instructor best. Years before, Glue would never have entertained the idea of watching *Godzilla vs. Kong*, but those days have passed— the days of being in Toronto with Elle and projecting on his living room wall the atmospheric films of Wong Kar-wai and the subtle movies of Hong Sang-soo. Glue even watched films by Godard back then. When Elle moved in, she brought her projector and the first night, they got high and watched *Twin Peaks*.

"What a weird show," Elle said. "This is making me think, Glue. If I ever come to visit you in Hong Kong, please don't feel like you need to come to the airport to pick me up."

What about this David Lynch TV show made Elle make such a statement?

"I need some space to myself, especially when I land. I always feel disoriented when I arrive at new places. I need to be ready to meet people. Especially after a flight. If I just see you there, waiting, being all excited, I'll be stressed out. It'll be bad for both of us. And, of course, picking people up is overrated. There's Uber."

The vibe of someone who is visiting a place and the vibe of someone who is returning to a place from vacation is similar. They feel too good about themselves.

Elle ended up visiting Glue in Hong Kong once, in July. This was when Glue was still a student in Canada, visiting his parents during the summer break. Elle stayed at the Novotel in Tung Chung, near Glue. Glue did not pick Elle up at the airport. They met at night, in the hotel lobby. Elle was happy to see Glue.

Nowadays, Glue has no one to watch such films with. He realizes that, without Elle, his patience for stylistic cinematography and intricate editing has dissipated.

One time, when the two were high, Glue suggested to Elle that they go to a rooftop. It was somewhere in the Junction in Toronto where Glue had overheard, when he was at a café, waiting for Elle, a couple on a date talking about how the stairs of the building could be accessed through the back door and that on the rooftop there, one can see the CN Tower between the residential buildings, and so, that night, they went. Glue and Elle had edibles an hour and thirty-five minutes before they arrived at the building, found the open door just as the edibles kicked in, and they took quite some time to get up the stairs. They were so high. And when they finally arrived at the rooftop, they lay down on the floor and looked up and the sky looked heavy and Glue's stomach growled and Elle couldn't stop laughing because the growling was loud and it didn't stop and there was nothing Glue could do.

Back to the film: Using his radioactive breath, Godzilla blasts a hole next to the Victoria Harbour that goes all the way to the middle of the earth and King Kong climbs out with a radioactive axe. King Kong slaps the ground and breaks a bunch of buildings in Wan Chai. Godzilla slams his tail and several more buildings crumble to the ground. They fight, breaking everything in Central. Kong jumps on an office building to dodge a radioactive blast by Godzilla before jumping back to Hong Kong Island; he takes off the top of the Hopewell Centre, uses it to fend off a blast by Godzilla before grabbing the axe to send Godzilla flying and falling on the Bank of China Tower.

Later tonight, the YouTube algorithm will recommend to Glue conspiracy videos, theorizing why Hong Kong is always being destroyed in films by Sony Pictures.

Godzilla gets up. Kong takes a crane and throws it at Godzilla. Godzilla strikes Kong with his tail. Buildings, from Causeway Bay to Wan Chai to Admiralty to Sheung Wan to Sai Ying Pun are destroyed. Godzilla steps on King Kong's chest. Bones crack.

Glue looks over at Po-Wing, who doesn't take his eyes off the screen. Godzilla breathes onto Kong's face and Kong growls and Godzilla growls back and steps harder on Kong's chest.

"Wait, I don't get it," says Glue. Why was King Kong fighting Godzilla to begin with?

Mechagodzilla bursts out from inside the Peak, breaking all the real estate in front of the mountain, and blasts red beans from its mouth, killing everyone in the Wan Chai Gap and the Magazine Gap before firing a bunch of missiles at Godzilla.

"'Cause big monsters fight, Glue, what do you want me to say?" says Po-Wing.

Anyways, Kong comes back to life because this white guy drives a plane into Kong's heart and the plane is actually a defibrillator and it brings Kong back to life. Emotional orchestral music plays and Kong slams his shoulder into a building, to fix his dislocated arm. The music crescendoes, becomes triumphant, nationalistic and proud, and King Kong teams up with Godzilla and Mechagodzilla to destroy Hong Kong Island. After a few minutes, Mechagodzilla is defeated and Godzilla dives into the South China Sea. Glue remembers listening to a national anthem and ejaculating into the same sea Godzilla is now diving into. Glue laughs.

Po-Wing frowns, acknowledging Glue's untimely laugh before saying, "Let's go downstairs for a beer."

*"MOTHERFUCKING MAINLANDERS,* coming here to buy all our shit." Po-Wing's mask is pulled down, resting on his chin. He spits on the floor. "Look! That one's carrying baby formula. See?"

Two women holding Mannings plastic bags walk towards the bus terminal.

"Up there, the communist baby formula they have, they're all fucked up, fucks their babies up, makes them weird and shit. Either that or they're too fucking expensive."

Glue frowns. Is this a communist problem?

Po-Wing flicks Glue's forehead.

"The fuck, dude."

"Aren't you mad, Glue? There's a rule that we can't buy more than two cans of baby formula at once now, you know? Shit changed after you left, I told you. You shouldn't have come back."

"Why do you care so much about baby formula?"

Po-Wing tries to flick Glue again.

"Stop it! Are you drunk already?" Glue's forehead hurts; he feels his dick tingling a little.

"Let me tell you, Glue. Everyone here is like me. They think like me. Not all of us say it out loud but most people here hate mainlanders. I'm just more upfront about it."

Glue takes another sip of beer. A group of airfield engineers, orange vests in hand, exit the 7-Eleven. When Glue first returned to Hong Kong, he was not used to the proximity between things. But getting used to this environment didn't take long. This is where Glue belongs. When they were eighteen, right before Glue left for Canada, Glue and Po-Wing had beers here. Glue and Po-Wing, almost ten years later, are sitting on the same stone staircase in front of the Tung Chung Post Office. Behind them, right across the street, is the Ngong Ping Cable Car and the Tung Chung Bus Terminal.

"Glue, let me tell you. There was this mainlander, right. He was in my lecture. He had this accent—"

"Dude, can you chill with the—"

"屌! (*Diu!*) Who the fuck are you to call me out?" Po-Wing's sudden change of tone frightens Glue. "You don't know what the fuck goes on here and now you come back trying to censor me? What the fuck do they feed you out West? You rich kids go to fucking Canada and sometimes you come back communists. Communist chink."

Glue's chink face becomes blank.

Po-Wing says this slowly, mouthing each word with every muscle on his face: "Communist chink."

Po-Wing's breath smells of wheat. He tries to flick Glue's forehead again.

"Stop it."

"It's so easy for you to judge us. Oh, you're so racist. So politically incorrect. Why do you hate your own kind? You have no idea what it's like here. This place used to be quiet. It's a suburb. Now there's that fucking bridge that goes to Macau, and a fucking cable car, and mainland tourists everywhere, and that outlet mall. You know what? Once, I saw a mainlander. He had a baby with him. He took off the baby's diaper, held the baby up, and let it shit on the street."

"What?"

"Don't believe me? Fuck you, Glen Wu. You don't know shit! This is not our home anymore. It's not what it used to be. If I were you, I would not have come back."

"Why do you keep saying that?"

"Privileged asshole. Why the fuck did you come back? To explore the opportunities your drama degree could get you? People here are trying to leave. And you? You came back to pretend to be an expat, to claim your honorary-white privilege."

"I'm not white," Glue murmurs.

"Oh, really now? I can see your chink face, Glue. But tell me. Did you finally get a full-time job? What's it like to be an ESL instructor?"

"Is that what this is about?" Glue has only told his mother about landing a job as an ESL instructor. After completing his certificate, he passed three rounds of interviews and landed a job earning the equivalent of CAN$50 an hour at Englishmentation, an online ESL company based in Hong Kong with over forty-five thousand students worldwide. Glue, who was a little surprised by how easy it was to become an ESL instructor, told his mother right away.

"Who told you that?" Glue asks Po-Wing.

"Gwen."

"You've been texting with Gwen?"

"I've always been in touch. You know how stressed out she is because of you?"

"That's not true." For some reason, this is making Glue jealous.

"It is."

"Stressed about what?"

"I was selling to her a while back. I think that Lester guy found her another dealer, though."

Glue is silent.

"What? I can't be talking to your sister, you ESL fuck? You think you'd be able to land that job if you didn't have a privileged life, if you didn't live abroad, if you didn't go to international school and shit? You're fucking dyslexic, Glue. If you were a local, you wouldn't even have passed any of our fucking standardized tests. You wouldn't have gone to university, and you wouldn't have the privilege to drop out from grad school just to come back to be an ESL instructor working from home."

Glue looks away.

"I was in an ESL class once, you know." Po-Wing takes another sip of beer. His tone is a tad calmer. "This Australian woman told me to repeat the phrase 'I saw sixty-nine farmers laughing on the phone.' She said I had an Asian accent, that I needed to practise saying this shit to get rid of it. I should repeat it in the morning, when I'm getting ready, when I'm showering, she told me. What the fuck does that even mean, though? Why do I see sixty-nine farmers laughing on the phone? Why are they laughing simultaneously? Are the farmers on the same call? Why am I being told to say this absurd shit? Why are there sixty-nine of them standing together, Glue? Is that what you tell your students? That there are sixty-nine farmers laughing on the phone?"

Glue lets out a soft and shameful chuckle.

"*Wai!* Don't ignore me, Glue. I'm asking you. Do you ask your students to say that there are sixty-nine farmers—"

Perhaps it's the alcohol. Otherwise Glue would never turn, clench his fist, and punch Po-Wing in the face—a direct blow. Po-Wing drops his beer. Yellow liquid spills from the silver can.

Glue is ready to throw hands.

Po-Wing buries his face between his thighs. "Why'd you punch me?" he murmurs. "That hurt, Glue. I don't like that." Po-Wing gets up. He picks up the knocked-over can and places it in the plastic bag. He opens another can of Sapporo. He doesn't look at Glue.

"I'm sor—"

Po-Wing slaps Glue so hard that he sees double. He grabs Glue and the two roll to the bottom of the short stone staircase outside the post office. The 7-Eleven's bright green, orange, and red lights illuminate the scene. Po-Wing is on top, holding Glue down with his weight, his hands clasping Glue's wrists. "Say it with me, Glen Wu." Po-Wing grins, showing his perfect teeth. "There are sixty-nine farmers—"

A construction worker walks by but doesn't even glance at the two.

Tears form in Glue's eyes. Po-Wing, still on top of him, doesn't notice that Glue is stimulating an erection in his pants. At least it doesn't seem to Glue that Po-Wing knows. Glue spits on Po-Wing's face and starts crying out loud. Po-Wing watches as tears run down Glue's greasy cheeks, two red palm marks forming on either side of his oily face.

"Ugh." Po-Wing helps Glue up. "Come over to mine."

GLUE NOTICES a *Joker* (2019) poster on Po-Wing's wall and next to the poster is a Captain America shield, the size of a wok, hanging, on the wall, above the Bang & Olufsen speakers. In addition to the pile of designer clothes on the couch, Glue also notices a stack of black-and-gold Fred Perry polo shirts, unworn, the plastic wrap and tags still intact.

"Why'd you buy so many of these?"

"They're pulling them from the shelves. I bought all the ones they had in stock."

Glue shivers. The cool air-conditioned room calms his dick down.

"Was it always this cold in here?"

"Fuck yeah," Po-Wing says. "Feels nice, doesn't it? Help yourself to a beer."

There used to be a variety of beer in the fridge, but these days, Po-Wing seems to drink only Sapporo and Blue Girl.

Po-Wing tosses Glue an ice pack. "Feel free to chill here

for a bit more, Glue. I'm just going to watch some YouTube or maybe a nineties movie."

"A nineties movie?"

"I'm thinking something by Stephen Chow, from the good old days. Maybe *The God of Cookery* or *From Beijing with Love.* Or maybe something by Wong Jing."

This director is notorious for his misogynistic B-movies.

"Maybe we can just watch some YouTube?" Glue says.

The night ends with Po-Wing falling asleep to political commentators on YouTube. There's something about Cambridge Analytica and Steve Bannon. Something about how Trump's international tactics and his deals with North American countries and the European Union will form a partnership that benefits the American economy. America First. The next video is by a YouTuber who goes by Stormtrooper, which in Chinese is 白兵 (direct translation: "White Soldier"). The video is titled "Hong Kong is the World's Testicles." "The world will survive without testicles," says Stormtrooper, "but cutting them off will hurt."

Po-Wing is falling asleep. For friends to remain friends, fights need to happen. Everything is okay. Glue mutes the video. With the sound off, Glue now notices what Stormtrooper is wearing—a navy blue hoodie that is a size too big. In the previous video, he wore a windbreaker of the same colour. Glue scrolls through the thumbnails—in each of them, the YouTuber wears navy blue. A rumour Glue once heard comes to mind. Maybe Stormtrooper isn't really supporting Western powers—that's too obvious.

Maybe Stormtrooper is paid to say everything he says—paid to celebrate America's tactics and look at the world only through the lenses of economics and politics. By promoting this celebrated and aggrandized version of America in Hong Kong, by polarizing the discourse—by framing everything as China vs. the US and siding with the US—he is aiming to promote and popularize the continuance of China's socialist market economy in this city. This thought gives Glue chills.

The streets are quiet in Tung Chung. The trees are still. There is a soft warm breeze, but the heat from earlier still lingers faintly on Glue's dry yet oily skin.

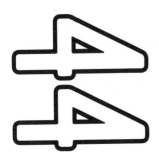

*IF I TURN RIGHT*, Glue thinks, *something good will happen when I return home*. Glue turns right, into a small garden; it is quite alright that it will take him longer to return home. *If I take a piss here, tomorrow will be a good day*. Glue looks around. It is dark. The streetlights are far away, illuminating the shopping mall and wet market at the end of this narrow path. Glue takes out his penis, and like a dog, with one leg on the ledge, he relieves himself on the sidewalk. He cannot see his own piss. He can smell it, though, and he hears the crisp sound of his urine hitting the stone pavement. Glue laughs. He didn't know his bladder had the capacity to hold so much beer. Piss continues to come out. He seldom urinates in public. Glue might be stepping in his own urine right now. The bottoms of his discounted Nike sneakers might be covered in his own piss, the smell of which he will probably be bringing back to his apartment, but he doesn't care. There are scratch marks on Glue's legs too, a result from the earlier fight with Po-Wing. This would be fine if Glue wore long pants, but since his return to Hong Kong, he's worn only shorts. It stings a little when droplets of his piss splash onto the scratches on his legs. But all is well. Glue turned right and took a piss; tomorrow will be a good day.

Maybe Po-Wing is right. Maybe Glue should never have returned to Hong Kong. Should he have stayed in Toronto? But that is far too simple, too didactic. Glue, these days, is often constipated.

When Glue returns home, he showers, tries to take a shit, can't, gives up, drinks whiskey, and gets into bed. He goes on YouTube again. The algorithm suggests a video about conspiracy theories behind the Godzilla film he just watched. Before the video starts, Glue watches a commercial for Sapporo, skips to the next commercial at the thirty-second mark, and watches a commercial for Blue Girl. To the left of the video is an ad for Dyson hand dryers. "Sony Pictures owns the rights to *Godzilla*, *King Kong*, and the *Pacific Rim* franchise," says one YouTuber, "all of which have scenes of monsters and robots destroying Hong Kong. All of these movies did well in mainland China. Hmmm. I wonder why." Is she suggesting that the US, Japan, and China want Hong Kong to collapse? Glue pours himself some more whiskey. He does not feel sleepy. But he should not watch YouTube any longer. Glue can feel, inside his mind, the forming of broken pieces of glass once more. He remembers the feeling of waking up that morning in June, when he met May at the bar downstairs from his apartment. A dark sea was inside his mind, the silent waves were making him nauseated. He keeps his eyes open. *Is this a sky? No, Glue, this is not a sky. This is a ceiling, a part of the apartment with the mortgage that you are responsible for paying.*

But until tomorrow, when Glue will teach his first ESL class, he can continue staring at this ceiling.

*IT IS THE* middle of September. Glue picked the perfect time to become an ESL teacher. Many expats left after the protests began. Why not go all out, Glue thinks. More is more. Glue decides to work as an IELTS examiner on weekends for extra cash.

After a full day of nonsense (teaching ESL is nonsense), Glue consumes more nonsense. He watches 微辣 Manner videos on YouTube. He watches reaction videos, too: Americans reacting to BTS; Koreans reacting to Americans reacting to BTS; BTS reacting to reactions of BTS (brought to you by BuzzFeed).

If you help the system, you get compensated; YouTubers make way more than you would expect. Glue is an ESL teacher and is finally, but slowly, getting compensated as well. It's a top-down system after all. This is true for most people: the more you do to perpetuate the stability of the ones above you, the more financially stable you become.

Glue has no problem living this way: consuming reaction

videos and the ads that come with them is simply part of his job as a person living in 2019. A few years ago, Glue was much more radical. Back then, he would certainly have resisted living such a life. He had concerns about the climate. Glue, along with Gwen and Elle, attended protests when they were students, in Toronto. Glue remembers, when he and Elle attended a climate protest, they saw a group of teenagers chanting, "Hey-ho! Justin Trudeau has to go!," criticizing the government for doing very little about the climate crisis other than planting a few trees. Glue had told Elle that Trudeau's government wasn't that bad compared to the situation in Hong Kong. "At least he looks like he cares" is what Glue said to Elle, who agreed.

But Glue is growing up. He is no longer naive and he will soon not be allowed to attend any protests because of the national security law. He is now an ESL instructor for Englishmentation, an online English-learning platform. He will now live the life of a real Hong Konger, a salary person, a conformist in this post-colonial space, in southern China, occupying the spaces of China's Guangdong–Hong Kong–Macau, China's Greater Bay Area, living the stereotype of a Hongkie, a person who speaks English, advantageous because of his white-adjacentness, and living life in order to make money and making money in order to live in the city where East meets West.

After completing his ESL certificate, Glue realized that his previous notion of making a stable living as a freelance translator, as someone with a drama degree, in Hong Kong was laughable. He would have been relying on his parents and Gwen all his life. Once again, Po-Wing was right. Why did Glue major in drama? Performing does not seem to suit his personality. But the years of attending music school had made Glue accustomed to performing onstage. Glue enjoyed, when he was an undergrad, watching plays and analyzing films and reading novels, but he was the only Chinese international student in the department, which, he now knows, was a bad sign. His sister and all of his friends were all a step ahead. They knew the truth about the world, and the truth about the world is learned in business school. If you choose the arts and humanities, capitalism tries to run you down. Or maybe Glue lacks talent. Maybe both. Teaching ESL doesn't take much talent. Like politicians reading from their teleprompters, Glue reads from slides written for him.

ESL, as a business, is mostly a scam. He remembers that, although English was the primary language at his high school, all the Canadian universities Glue applied to, seeing that he was from Hong Kong, asked him to take the IELTS test again. He had taken the test when he transferred to the Queen's Music Academy, but his results had expired. Yes—according to IELTS, every two years you forget how to speak the world's most dominant language. The best way to help language learners perfect a language is to have them write a test that has nothing to do with writing or reading or fluency in a language—whatsoever. IELTS is perverse. It does not believe in growth. The entire test is about reading one pointless passage after another and checking answers that are all equally meaningless. It is necrophilic. It costs CAN$300 to take. If IELTS had sex organs, it'd be aroused by corpses. IELTS would be fucking dead bodies.

Canadian universities also require students to have community involvement hours in high school. Even as a teen living in a hyper-capitalist special economic region, Glue, when he saw this requirement, was troubled. Isn't framing something as volunteer work just capitalism making an excuse for not compensating work that is actually doing something for the community? But again, he is no longer naive. He accepts that this is also a reality of the world—volunteer work and serving the community is not work worthy of payment. Though he was upset about this requirement back then, he completed his volunteer hours, working as a basketball coach's assistant, recording stats of his team's players at the local YMCA. Then, he got what he wanted.

**EACH DAY** is a repetition of the last. When Glue gets tired of reaction videos, he starts drinking. He watches porn when he can't sleep. If, when he wakes up, there is whiskey in the glass next to him still, he downs it before rolling back into bed. After the third alarm, he gets out of bed and turns on the webcam.

"Repeat after me," Glue says. "It's Saturday. We do not have to volunteer at the firm."

"It's Saturday. We do lot have to volunteer at the farm."

"Very good, Kyoko," Glue says, not bothering to correct Kyoko's mistakes. Glue also doesn't shave or wash his face before work. He downloaded a beauty filter to make himself look presentable enough. His breath smells of whiskey and vomit, but no one knows this. He might have had congee for dinner last night.

"Why are you still going to the firm, Kyoko?"

"I want the more work experience in the workplace tomorrow."

Englishmentation designed all the material. Not just the business of ESL but even the content that Glue teaches serves to further stabilize the classes above. But that's okay. Glue is getting paid. And perhaps because he is getting paid, he is no longer that bothered by May's having stolen something of his. He is stealing from others as well, he feels. He is taking home a monthly salary by taking advantage of a system that requires international students to pay a large sum to take a test. He is a less honest thief compared to May.

It has been close to a month since Glue has seen May. Glue misses May but since they failed to have sex last time and that failing to have sex made him like May more, he feels embarrassed by the idea of contacting May. It has also been a while since Glue and Po-Wing last met. Which means Glue is running out of weed. He's drinking more.

Po-Wing and Glue have been friends since the two were in the second grade. They don't have much in common but they lived in the same area as kids. Like atoms, proximity and nothing else seems to have brought them together. Glue remembers being slapped by Po-Wing. "I saw sixty-nine farmers laughing on the phone." Po-Wing was asked to say this in order to rid him of his Asian accent.

"Kyoko, say this with me," Glue says to his thirteen-year-old student. "There are sixty-nine farmers laughing on the farm."

"There are sixty-nine fama laughing on the fam."

"Good. One more time, Kyoko."

Glue smirks as he watches Kyoko repeat the phrase. Glue sips his coffee, which, earlier, he spiked with rum.

**IN THE** middle of October, amidst the height of the pro-democracy protests, Glue will remember that at one point he wanted to write poems. At one point, Glue remembers, he showed glimpses of talent, even published something during his time as a graduate student in creative writing.

Glue attempts writing again.

**Chinks, bro~**
October 2019

**Chinks #1**
The flashlight button on the dropdown menu of my
home screen forms human chains on Lion Mountain.
(It's Lion Rock, in English, on Google Maps.)[5]

**Chinks #2**
Mid-Autumn Festival lights celebrate lanterns that take
the form of Ultraman's red face.

**BROS**
rooftops (are romantic) and also
            blockchain(s).


LEGS
And there is a bookshelf between the dudes and me
and the book *Baby Massage and Yoga: Volume 1* is yellow
and so am I and the people across are talking about how
their legs become numb when they are on long-distance

---

5

flights and they might be on a date and they might be friends on a date, and I realize, and this is not really a realization, that I could have lasted longer last night if I had done more sit-ups and crunches and if I had drunk more water and stretched before and afterwards.

These are terrible. But it is quite all right that Glue can no longer write poems. Poetry does not matter. Poetry cares too little about grammar, and because of that, poems are useless to ESL students.

**48**

*GLUE IS* bouncing his left leg below the table.

"Have you been seeing anyone?" Gwen asks.

"Why you ask?" Glue has a toothpick in his mouth.

It is three in the afternoon and the two are just having coffee. Gwen looks at Glue, confused, as though she is wondering why Glue needs to pick his teeth. Do they even give out toothpicks at Starbucks?

"Just wondering." Amidst all this pollution and humidity, Gwen's hair looks neat and clean, shoulder-length and straight. "It's been a while since you saw anyone long-term."

"Not as lucky as you, *ah mah*. You happy *lah*. How's Lester Tse?"

"He's looking to start his own business on the side," Elle says, ignoring Glue's fake Chinglish accent.

"What the business?"

"Can you stop doing that with your leg? The table's wobbling."

"Sor." Glue nods his head slightly to accompany this Chinglish expression.

Gwen frowns a deep frown. "It's an imaginary— I mean, immigration consultancy. He said a friend of his from Toronto came here and they have this idea that they should help people migrate to Canada."

In Hong Kong, in October, the weather can be hot. When it's hot, conversations often skip from one topic to another. "Has Lester been to the Tian Tan Buddha?" Glue asks, staring at the long line of people waiting to see the statue.

Backpacks come in all colours. From the Starbucks patio where they're seated, they see tourists with bucket hats lining up next to the floor fountain to get on the cable car.

"When he first got here, he had this idea that we should pretend to be tourists."

"He *is* a tourist."

"*He is a tourist.*" Gwen slants her eyes slightly, mimicking Glue's. "Lester wore a camera around his neck and he put on a fedora. He said he was going to spend the day as 'Asian Mraz.' That's how it went down." Gwen told Glue that she found Lester's lack of self-awareness, and his total self-assurance, cute.

"We spoke English to everyone that day. People seemed nicer to us."

Glue switches the topic again. "Have you seen *Love in a Puff?*"

"Love in a what?" Gwen frowns for the third time this afternoon.

"It's this Kong-made rom-com."

"No."

Glue knows this—Gwen hasn't seen a Kong-made film since she was a teenager. She would sometimes watch Korean or Japanese films with Glue and Elle back when they watched films on that white wall in Toronto, but Kong-made films never interested Gwen. "A rom-com, too? When did you start watching those?"

"There's this scene. A guy and a woman in a park. They see a snail on a fence, so they stop to fuck with it."

Gwen rolls her eyes at this. "Where is this going, Glue?"

"The guy drops his cigarette when he tries to flick the snail and then a security guard shows up so the guy pretends to be Japanese to get away from a littering fine and the woman bows and pretends to be Korean. They walk away, right, but the woman's phone rings, and the ringtone is this Cantonese bot so the guard gets mad, learning that they're locals, and runs after them."

Gwen doesn't laugh. "Have you just been watching random trashy movies all the time?"

"Just thought that was a funny scene," says Glue.

"Well, it's true," Gwen says. "The Japanese do get away with things."

Gwen is right. Glue knows that the reason why the man in *Love in a Puff* (2010) was (almost) able to get away from the guard is because the Japanese state is good at employing marketing tactics to promote themselves as "civilized" citizens, "good" tourists. The Japanese government even established a US$500 million Cool Japan Fund using tax-payer money to increase Japan's soft power. Think of Japan. J-A-P-A-N. It's fashionable. It is cute and cool and clean and has badass ninjas and samurai and shows on Netflix and delicious sushi and the hipster capitalism of Haruki Murakami—jazz records and whiskeys and cats and monkeys and shit. Japan is so good at PR that its existence in the minds of people around the world becomes effectively detached from its previous involvement in the Second World War. Now, Glue thinks, they do what they want. Hold the Olympics amidst a pandemic? Sure. What about dumping nuclear waste into the sea? Why not? Detain racial minorities? After you, China—I mean, Guantanamo Bay. Oh, the comfort women were not slaves? Of course they weren't. The Nanjing Massacre never happened as well? Well, okay then. Revise history. Do even more marketing. Learn from Yukio Mishima—self-Orientalize—be so Japanese that you kill yourself. Shed Asia, Join Europe! In the LAND OF THE RISING SUN, the sense of national superiority needs to be internalized, too. It needs to be certain, hammered down; some Japanese, today, do not even consider themselves Asian. The Japanese state plans on upping their game as well. Japan's Moonshot project, named after a previous project undertaken by the US (of course), seeks to collect citizens' data and wants to have each Japanese citizen, by 2050 or so, upload their cognitive information to up to ten avatars. The government is attempting to multiply Japanese national identity. With a life's worth of data from every citizen, the Japanese state can practically eliminate the death of the Japanese people. Information can live forever. Identity is information with self-awareness. All the government has to do is upload "you" (your data, up to the point of your physical death) to a machine that thinks it is you. Thus, Japanese national identity lives on; it can also be kept fully intact (in the sense that identities are saved as "Japanese" data and will therefore always be "Japanese"), solving the issue of the nation's population decline without taking in immigrants. In this scenario, a Japanese person (or at least a Japanese person's identity) can work forever for the state. Japan is a self-proclaimed homogeneous nation, after all. This would solidify that claim even further.

The colonization of life (removing death from life): this is perhaps the ultimate form of violence.

**"GIVE KONG-MADE** films a try. Turn your brain off. It's a good way to unwind."

Gwen looks bored. "Nope. The directors are always men and they tend to make the women in those movies just as toxic as men. But I guess that's just a Kong dude's idea of equality. I don't need to watch that."

Glue wonders if that is his idea of equality as well.

"You should visit the salon," Gwen tells him. "You need a perm. The top of your head's looking a bit flat."

Gwen's comment reminds Glue of Elle. The only piece of writing he has ever published featured a scene where Elle tells him that his head is flat and that he should avoid wearing hats, a scene that is plausible but a fictitious one nonetheless. Glue finds it funny that Elle would say such a thing. He also feels vulnerable when such things are said to him. And when Glue feels vulnerable, he falls in love.

Glue looks down at his iced Americano, the melting ice, clear water rising to the surface of the brown fluid. This cost him HK$40. He takes a sip of the watery coffee. Given the housing prices in this jam-packed city, when one purchases a coffee, most of what is paid—minus the plastic cup, green straw, and the watery brown liquid—just goes towards Starbucks's rent, which is paid to the mall, which is owned by the property developers, which has deals with the local government, which owns most of the land and rents it out to foreign investments—and this is one of the many reasons why everything here is so expensive. Hong Kong is run like a corporation. We don't have a mayor or a premier. Like a company, we've got this chief executive appointed by the Central People's Government. We rely on tourism and trade, and exist as a tax haven, and, like most corporations, we don't give a shit about the poor. The elimination of sales tax does nothing for locals; it only serves to benefit the one percent and tourists. Which is to say, it is not just on the local level that we treat tourists better—all of this is carefully designed; Hong Kong is where businesses invest. The system is built this way; it thinks outwardly, prioritizes wealthy foreigners. This is why the idea of America First appeals to so many here.

"I'm going blond, gonna change things up a little, you know." Glue runs his fingers through his flat, greasy hair.

"Don't go blond, Glue." Gwen doesn't even look at Glue when she says this.

The patio is getting crowded. Like bored telemarketers waiting for someone to pick up the phone, people are waiting for seats to open up in this outdoor sauna.

"Have we been here for twenty minutes already?" Gwen asks.

"Think so. My free Wi-Fi just got cut off."

Gwen gets up to leave.

"The mortgage. I think I can handle a larger portion starting this month," Glue says. "Plus, Mom and Dad are paying still, so—"

"It's okay. You just started a new job. And I am still a co-owner."

*Love in a Puff* (2010) is actually the first film of a trilogy. The series ends with the woman meeting two aliens at the Tai Lam Chung Dam. The UFO doesn't land. It hovers above the dam. Two aliens beam down from it. The aliens, after doing some math, tell the woman that there is a 50 percent chance that her relationship with the guy who likes to fuck with snails will work out. She decides to get back together with the guy. Happy ending.

**MAYBE GLUE** is still drunk; later that week he finds himself speaking Chinglish to some white Americans and a couple of South Asian guys at the basketball court.

"I next. I next," Glue says. "*Wai!* Nice meet you, bro. I Glen Wu. Da friends call me Glue," he tells the guys on his team and gives each of them a high-five. "*Wai!* Bro, you on my team?" Glue says to a skinny Caucasian kid.

"Yeah, man."

"He too? The guy in da red? He on our team, too?"

"Yup, I'm on your team, bro."

"Cool. I guard this guy," Glue says, pointing at the tall Indian man in front of him. Glue's opponent, several inches taller, can't help but chuckle at his defender, a lanky chink with a chink accent.

"Let go. Ball in, bro."

MAY, on a Saturday evening, asks Glue to come to her apartment. Glue goes without hesitation. This time, Glue is sure he can get an erection. When May tells Glue to fuck her from behind, Glue slips on his AirPods. The lights are off. A Spotify playlist composed of only national anthems plays in his ears. His back, which often aches from long hours of sitting, seems not to bother him. He fucks industriously, brass instruments playing inside his brain. *I can fuck forever.* That is not true. When he's about to ejaculate, his muscles tense up. Glue leans forward, lifts May's body, and bites May's shoulder before letting out all the cum his prick could muster. May lets out a cry. The neighbour next door knocks on the wall. "Shut the fuck up!"

Glue tosses his headphones on the floor before collapsing onto the bed.

"What was that?" May asks.

"Your neighbour."

"I think something fell on the floor."

Glue touches May's sweaty back and then her shoulder, feeling the spot he bit into. "Sorry." Glue kisses the bite mark. This feels necrophilic. Glue licks the bite mark.

"There's a bottle of aloe gel under the bed," says May.

Glue applies the cooling gel to May's shoulder, soothing the redness. The smell of May's sweat mixed with the fragrance of her shampoo makes his penis tingle. He discreetly strokes his dick a few times.

"Did it feel good?" Glue wants to know if the sex was pleasurable for May, but it sounds like he's asking about the cooling gel.

"Can you go get us some weed?" says May instead of answering. "I want to get high."

**GLUE DRAGS** himself to Po-Wing's apartment.

"Hey, hey, hey, motherfucker. Ran out of weed?"

"Yeah," says Glue. "Sorry to bother you."

"That's a terrible movie," says Po-Wing. "*Sorry to Bother You*. I don't get that movie."

After the subjectively intense sexual experience underscored by triumphant music, Glue, though he enjoyed the absurdist comedy Po-Wing is referencing, is much too tired to defend it. "Can I have some water, please?"

A YouTube video is playing on Po-Wing's Samsung 65" 4K UHD HDR Curved LED Tizen Smart TV. Hong Kongers are being asked if they would consider moving to the UK. "Young people say they would continue fighting for Hong Kong's freedom in England," says a man in his thirties. "I don't think they should. That's like mainlanders bringing their mainland values here when they move. I think, if you move, you should just move. Just focus on becoming British. Why are you fighting for something that has nothing to do with the locals? That'll just make life difficult there."

Po-Wing tosses Glue a bottle of Evian.

"Would you move to England?" the interviewer asks.

"So long as I still get access to Facebook and Google and stuff and I'm not forced to use any of those Chinese apps, I'm just gonna stay here."

"Isn't the TV a bit too loud?" Glue says. The door is open. Only the metal gate is closed. "Won't your neighbours complain?"

"Nah. The ones next door, they go drag racing every night. No one cares. If someone's upset, they can move out. Good luck finding another place to live." Po-Wing laughs at his own cynicism. "Wanna chill here for a bit? I got some Sapporo."

"I got to go, man. Next time."

Po-Wing fills the small transparent ziplock bag with weed. "That'll be a thousand." Po-Wing's voice, which a moment ago was friendly, now sounds stern. This sudden shift in tone is familiar. Glue remembers Mrs. Angela, an English teacher of his at the Queen's Music Academy. She married a white British man, an ex-military living in Hong Kong. She changed her last name to Schmitt. She would shift her tone drastically to intimidate her students, friendly one moment, sarcastic the next, like Anne Robinson in that British game show. Mrs. Angela—she preferred students call her by her first name—attacked her students with the same kind of snobbishly British absolutism.

The cause is the consequence. Glue takes out three red

one-hundred-dollar notes from his wallet—how much he usually pays.

"I said a thousand, Glue."

"You drunk? Come on, man. Just—"

"Gotta adjust for inflation, Glen Wu. It's a thousand. You want it?"

"Dude, come on. I got to go—"

"You got the money with you or not?"

"Is something wrong?"

"Oh no." Po-Wing throws his hands up when he says this, his palms facing forward, animated. He looks like a character being confronted by a police officer in a light-hearted anime series. "Do you know another person in Tung Chung who can get you grass, Glen Wu?" Po-Wing extends his right hand, his palm open. "If not, you're gonna have to pay up, buddy."

"Are we good?"

"We are good, Wu Sir. I'm just doing business here. Now, you going to pay up or not?"

*Sir*—a title reserved for teachers in Hong Kong, police-men, and the rich Hong Kongers knighted by the Queen.

"Fine." Glue takes two bronze-coloured five-hundred-dollar bills from his wallet.

"Ah. I knew it, Wu Sir. You've got some dough now. Got that ESL money. How does it feel?"

"Where's the weed?"

Po-Wing tosses the weed on the floor; small nuggets of it fall out of the bag. "Oops."

The two chinks stare at the bag on the floor between them. The interviews continue in the background.

"You gonna pick that up, Glue?"

*We have colonial ties with Great Britain.*

"You're the one who dropped it," says Glue.

*Western democracies, we need your support.*

"Fine," Po-Wing says.

*We want a national anthem, a song that belongs to us, just us.*

Po-Wing squats, looks at the weed, and blows on it softly. Po-Wing looks up, smiles at Glue with his perfectly white teeth. "Fucking pussy-ass chink," says Po-Wing. "Really? I just took your money and threw your weed on the ground and you're just gonna walk away?" Po-Wing laughs. "Wu Sir, you're gonna be a fucking ESL instructor your whole life."

Being called "Sir" is much too triggering for this former social justice warrior, who, if he had stayed in Toronto, would be advocating to defund the police. The moment Glue turns around, Po-Wing slaps him in the face and kicks him in the balls—a fast and strong kick—too quick for Glue to react. "Wooo!" Po-Wing shrieks, looking ecstatic from having just kicked a self-righteous chink in the balls. Pain shoots from Glue's testicles all the way to the top of Glue's head, making him nauseated. Glue is on his knees, trying to feel his testicles with his palms. But Po-Wing is far from done. He slaps Glue once more, even harder this time, on the same side of his face. For a moment Glue cannot hear a thing through his left ear. Curled up like a worm, Glue is on the floor, hands clutching his testicles, sweating all over, unable to utter a word. Po-Wing pulls the hem of his own crewneck shirt all the way to his chin, showing his abs, looking like a character straight out of *Dragon Ball Z*. Po-Wing also lights a cigarette, jittering his leg—the body language of a triad member, the ones with greasy hair found in Kong-made films from back in the good old days, back when Hong Kong was a British colony. The golden age of cinema, they called it—the aesthetic that Quentin Tarantino would rip off and win Oscars for. A couple nights later, Glue will watch *Paprika* (2006) when he's having trouble sleeping. Glue will notice that Christopher Nolan's *Inception* (2010) is a white remake of the Japanese anime.

Po-Wing kicks Glue in the stomach. The kick is deep. Glue spits out a bit of blood and coughs. Cigarette still in his mouth, Po-Wing opens the metal gate and drags Glue into the hallway. He places the two five-hundred-dollar bills on the ground, right next to Glue's face. "Communist chink," he murmurs, before picking up the bag of weed and tossing it at Glue.

Glue pulls down his mask and tries to spit at Po-Wing, but his mouth is dry. His saliva does not land anywhere near his target.

Curled up so tight, Glue looks as if he's shrinking, like the tiny shrimp found in a har gow. He lies outside the government-subsidized apartment's metal gate and feels tears in his eyes.

Po-Wing shakes his head. "I don't remember ever crying. I'm sure I did as a child, but I don't remember. I've made you cry twice this week." He shuts the gate, leaves the wooden door open.

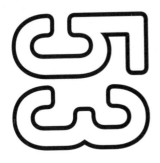

WHEN GLUE is finally able to get up, he walks back into the apartment and sees Po-Wing asleep, next to a pile of designer clothes. In front of him is a glorious mess— empty cans of beer, cigarette butts, and ashes are spread all over the glass coffee table. Po-Wing's apartment, its air conditioning on full blast, is the temperature of Canada in October. Feeling cool and hot air run through his body simultaneously, Glue sneezes, which hurts his balls and stomach. Glue leaves the door open and shuffles down the hallway, half a step at a time. At the end of the hallway, a woman leaves her apartment, glances at Glue, and walks away. Glue can still hear Po-Wing's YouTube videos playing through his Bang & Olufsen speakers: *You need enough money to support yourself for at least four to seven years.* The YouTube commentators are now discussing the process of immigrating to the UK. *The more degrees and work experience you have, the better. Same with moving to Canada.*

Will Glue be stuck here, for the rest of his life, in Tung Chung, paying his mortgage? His mortgage makes it difficult for him to return to his empty apartment. No longer does he want to stare at the white ceiling in his room. But everything is okay because the 7-Eleven next to the post office is where he belongs. He should tell May that he will not return to her place tonight. But Glue cannot muster the mental energy to check his phone.

"Anything to go with the beer?" asks the clerk.

Glue picks up the six-pack of San Miguel. "Two packs of Marlboro, the mentholated black ones, and a lighter."

"Three hundred and twenty—"

Glue taps his Octopus card on the machine and leaves the store.

Two cans of the golden beer stand between Glue's legs, pressing against his balls. This eases the pain a little. At two thirty in the morning, finally able to feel his testicles again, Glue messages May, asks her to meet him here if she's awake. He does this after asking a passerby to unlock his phone for him. "Turn off the data and swipe away all of the notifications, if you don't mind." He also finishes two beers and three cigarettes on the staircase outside the post office.

There is a yellow bus, a double-decker, on it an ad— BEA, Bank of East Asia. With only four passengers inside, it heads to the airport. On the ad,[6] the handsome Shawn Yue, who also plays the guy who fucks with snails, is in a trench coat, standing amongst some trees, his back facing the camera. He turns his head, gazing at Glue, mesmerized by what he's seeing. The large white characters on the bus read DON'T JUST BE RICH, BE WEALTHY.

Glue's face is cut, his hair is wet, and sweat is seeping through his white linen T-shirt.

"What the fuck happened to you?" May's white Nike windbreaker is zipped all the way up and she's in flip-flops.

"Beer?" Glue's throat, dried from smoking consecutive cigarettes, cracks, making him sound like a pubescent boy.

"I'm gonna get us some water first."

May pours the entire contents of a bottle of Watsons Water over Glue's head.

"Shit!" Glue shrieks. He tries to open his eyes. "Fuck me."

"Feels good, doesn't it?"

It does. Glue, for a brief second, feels like a basketball player being celebrated by his teammates after hitting the

---

6

game-winning shot. But, like drinking Red Bull, the excitement soon passes, leaving Glue feeling heavy.

May pops open a can of San Miguel and lights one of the cigarettes. They can even see it from here, the gleaming lights from the Hong Kong International Airport. Hong Kongers need to catch their red-eye flights. It is never fully dark here; too many streetlights illuminate the roads.

"I read your writing," May says.

"What?"

"I read 'Deeping Yellows.'"

Glue smiles, which hurts his face. But Glue, right now, has no desire to discuss what he wrote back then. All he wants to do is to smoke and drink and dwell quietly, in an inebriated state, in front of the humid lights of this 7-Eleven logo.

"Do you write still?"

Glue shakes his head. Back at Po-Wing's, when Glue was finally able to get up on two legs, he took the weed with him—but he only took one of the five-hundred-dollar bills; the other he slipped back into Po-Wing's apartment. At that moment, he felt that to be the right thing to do. Self-righteous much?

"Wanna put a bit of this in our cigs?" Glue takes out the small transparent plastic bag. The bag is full. Po-Wing must have picked up everything that fell out of it. "We can just smoke here."

"Not afraid of the po-po?"

"They only fuck with locals. Just don't speak Canto,"

Glue says, recalling Lester Tse's character—Asian Mraz. "Pretend to be a tourist or something."

So the two smoke the weed with their mentholated cigarettes and wash the burning sensation down with San Miguel.

Glue looks down at the two cans of beer between his legs.

May finishes her joint. She rests her head on Glue's shoulder. Glue slips the five-hundred-dollar bill into May's jacket pocket. He's not sure why he does this.

It is warm. Glue has not experienced such a warm October since he left for Canada to study when he was eighteen.

Time slows down when it's hot.

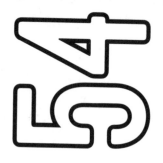

# Deeping Yellows

July 2018

*by Glen Wu*

I light a joint, which is illegal. Getting high in the shower with me is a bucket. The bucket is upside down. My phone is playing the song "Tong Poo" (1978). Warm water from the shower lands on the back of my neck, runs down my chest, and drips from the tip of my penis onto the bucket, making an empty sound. Years later, I hear the same sound in a documentary, *Ryuichi Sakamoto: Coda* (2017). In one scene, Sakamoto is seen standing in the rain holding a bucket over his head and listening to the sound of the rain landing on the bucket. His bucket is blue. Mine is yellow.

It is the summer of 2014. I am a student studying drama in Canada, currently visiting my parents in Hong

Kong over the break. This is Tung Chung, where I grew up, ten minutes from the Hong Kong International Airport. There is an outlet mall downstairs where mainland Chinese tourists shop for discounted goods before their flights. Luxury goods are more expensive in mainland China. I've never bought anything from the mall. Perhaps because it's too close to where I live.

I became a teacher. "Please take out a piece of paper and try to translate the music you're about to hear into words," I tell my class. "Just write whatever comes to your mind." I connect my laptop to the sound system and play "Tong Poo" on Spotify.

One of my students writes:

| | | | |
|---|---|---|---|
| I hate this song. | I ate this song. | I late this song. | I Kate this song. |
| I mate this song. | I date this song. | I Cate this song. | I rate this song. |
| I Yates this song. | I pate this song. | I sate this song. | I fate this song. |
| I gate this song. | I bate this song. | I Nate this song. | |

It reminds me of Zelda.

| | | |
|---|---|---|
| I want to fuck Zelda. | Hard. | I hate this song. I want *Zelda* to fuck *me*. |

The song, "Tong Poo," reminds me of something my hairdresser once told me. A friend of his started a business—a small place in the middle of Shinjuku—for people to take naps. People usually visit around three in the afternoon—the best time to nap. He tells me all of this while I am getting a perm. My hairdresser removes a curler from my head.

You once told me, with genuine concern, that my head was too flat. "More volume on the top will make you look better," you said. You also recommended that I avoid hats. "You look terrible with hat hair," you said.

I look at myself in the mirror at the hair salon. There are thirteen curlers on my head; eight of them are pink, and none of them are yellow. You also told me once that I'd look terrible bald. My hair uncurls from one of the pink curlers. I imagine myself standing in the rain, holding a bucket over my head, listening, and hoping that I don't go bald.

The lyrics to "Tong Poo" are sparse. In fact, the nine lines don't come in until halfway through the song. "Tong Poo" is considered disco music. I find out that when he was writing the song Ryuichi Sakamoto was inspired by Chinese classical music and the Cultural Revolution (whatever that means). But who the fuck is Tong Poo? At some point the singer sings, "Feel me come!"; what does that mean? Tong Poo only exists in the song. And Ryuichi Sakamoto has been diagnosed with oropharyngeal cancer.

*I hate this song. I ate this song. I late this song. It reminds me of Zelda.*

Which Zelda? Fitzgerald? The one I want to fuck? The character in the Nintendo game?

I go home to Toronto, to a condo. It is small. You are not home. I think about giving you a call to ask where you are, to see if I should prepare dinner for us. I am also eager to tell you what Mindy from London, Ontario, submitted for the exercise. I hear a beep. The dishes are clean. I forget to call you. I open the dishwasher. Steam emerges. The dishwasher is empty. I check the upper rack and then the lower one. All I find is a single chopstick. It is made of wood. It is warm.

*About the author:*

**Glen Wu** (he/him, born 1993, Hong Kong, SAR, China) is an MFA candidate at the University of Guelph's creative writing program. He holds a B.A. in drama from the University of Toronto, and a B.Ed. from York University. Glen also works as a part-time English teacher at Atlantia Education. After completing his MFA, Glen wishes to teach creative writing and drama at the secondary level.

**Contact:** glenwuglue@outlook.com

# HEAVIER

# THAN A

五

# DEATH IN

# THE FAMILY

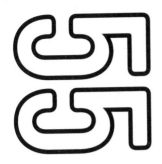

**PERHAPS IT'S** because they're both dressed like they live upstairs, May in flip-flops and Glue in slides. The police officers who walk by don't even glance at them. But to be safe, they decide to leave, putting the remaining beers in the plastic bag.

May separates the recyclables from the disposables. "I feel like I might want to leave Hong Kong soon."

"I see," Glue says. "I sometimes have the urge to leave as well." Glue doesn't tell May that he is beginning to feel that he can get used to it here. "Want to walk to the harbourside?" Glue's eyes are red from the weed.

The cable cars swing above the water. The blue speedboats, tied to the shore, move up and down with the waves, their orange life buoys hanging on the sides.

May chuckles. "Sorry, I tend to find more things funny when I'm high." May tells Glue she's thinking about a tweet she glossed over this morning.

"What's the tweet?" Glue asks.

"The UK, America, and China want to fuck so they use

Hong Kong as a condom." Right when May says this, she looks as though she regrets telling Glue about the tweet. The rules they established when they first started sleeping together still stand. Rule one—don't talk politics.

"That's more sad than funny, actually," says Glue. Glue's face hurts. He is staring at the polluted water.

"I've been thinking," says May. "A while ago, I couldn't stop looking at images and videos of the protests. Now, looking back, I feel as if time, for me, back then, was moving in all directions. It's like I was in a disembodied state of consciousness. I felt transparent. I was watching those activist leaders in exile giving speeches overseas, in the UK, right? Have you seen those?"

Glue shakes his head, which is a lie. Of course he has seen those when he was scrolling through Instagram Reels at night.

"They had all these speeches in Australia, the US, and even Japan, quoting Gandhi and Shakespeare. One guy is in exile in England right now. But I can't help but wonder, with so many people who have BNO passports wanting to leave Hong Kong for England, if he is really in exile or if he is finally free."

May is right. If what you want is freedom and freedom is sought through your proximity to whiteness, then living in exile, in the United Kingdom, you are free as can be. Those on the ground, here, not famous, not infamous, the less assimilated, less important, filled with anger, are arrested, continue to be arrested.

"Anyways, Glue. Sorry. I know we said we wouldn't talk politics. I'm sorry for not responding to your messages back then."

They do not talk politics—this is the first rule they have. The second rule is that they do not have to answer questions if they do not want to. Glue made the first rule and May made the second.

May thinks for a bit before asking this: "Don't feel like you need to answer me. I just feel I should ask. What happened to your face?"

Glue, all of a sudden, has the urge to ask May if "May" is her real name, but the pain in his groin is too much. Glue doesn't ask. It is almost four in the morning. "I've never been here this late," Glue says.

May doesn't seem to mind not knowing why Glue was limping, had two cold cans of beer between his legs, and why his face is swollen. "You know what bothers me, Glue? There are two things in the world that bother me. One. My parents. Two. People with a false sense of security. Maybe the two are related."

"Why is that?"

"Behind all stability is just chaos. Everything that appears stable is based on nothing. Money is created by banks when they make loans to people who are already in financial need, those who feel they need to own property, or people who are ignorant enough to believe they can become rich one day. Actually, that might not be entirely accurate. Money is also circulating government debt. If money is anything, it is debt, and debt is something with a negative value. So, what do we do, living in societies where the primary mode of exchange is based on negative value?"

Glue chugs some of the beer from one of the cans between his thighs. May is speaking too fast. Glue's balls still ache. He is in no state to discuss the philosophy of money. "Can I lie on your lap, May? You can continue talking." Glue lies down, sideways, his ear pressing against May's sweaty lap.

"Glue. Everything collapses. Everything is just made up. We are not our brains. We are just stories our brain tells ourselves. And all we do is tell ourselves stories to train ourselves to perform stability to the best of our abilities. That's why we are able to work and assimilate. We're all just pretending that all of this will never collapse."

May is right. Capitalism is maintained by nothing but collective performative acts of stability that protect the status quo. We're surprisingly good at this. Too good, actually; it has become much easier to imagine the end of the world than it is to imagine the end of capitalism.

**"MY PARENTS** don't know I'm here, you know?" May tells Glue to get up, that his head is too heavy and that her legs are becoming numb. She passes Glue another beer.

Glue is not too surprised by this. Glue and May never talked about their families. "Where do they think you are?"

"Still in Sussex. You heard of Sussex? I don't think a lot of people here have heard of Sussex. It's quite nice there. It's a little too quiet for me, though."

"Where are they?"

"They're here," May says. "They live in the New Territories. I told you they raised me religious, but they're not exactly Christian. They're a little extreme. They believe that God is going to bring an end to Hong Kong soon, said something about there being a holy war here after the first mass protest. So after I graduated, they made sure that I stayed in the UK. They even kept my HKID. Isn't that a bit much? They took my ID!"

"Wait. So you don't have an ID?" What if, earlier, the police had asked for the two to show their IDs?

May takes out her cardholder, showing Glue an ID card. The name on it reads Rachel Ai-Ming Anderson. Anderson? Rachel's hair is tied into a bun, exactly the same as May's. But if one looks closely, one will notice that this is not May but another woman, roughly the same age but with slightly Caucasian features. "If I speak English when cops ask me questions, they let me go. It's happened many times. I feel a little guilty but I still do it. I don't feel like I'm self-colonizing when I'm using Hong Kong's colonial history to get out of government control."

Glue returns the card to May. "Whose is this?"

"A friend of mine's. She invited me to live with her after I told her I haven't been back since high school. But right when I got here, her parents told her to move in with them in Toronto. They didn't want her to be in Hong Kong with all the riots. She didn't want to live with them but she still feels like she needs to obey her parents' wishes somehow. So when she left, she gave me her HKID in exchange for the keys to my place in Sussex. We switched! The apartment I live in belongs to her parents."

Glue doesn't know if any of this is true. Didn't May visit Yangshuo a few months ago? Glue thinks about asking her how it is possible to travel so easily and come back using someone else's ID but decides not to. He's asking too many questions already. Glue doesn't even know if May is her real name. He takes another swig of beer and as the cold beer slides down his throat, in a moment of sudden sober-ness, he remembers what May said that time he was con-stipated, that if she could create a simulated reality, it would be one where Christianity does not exist. "And this cult your parents are in," Glue asks. "It's a Christian one?"

"It's derived from it. So many religions come from Christianity. But the one they're in, it's this end-of-the-world cult. I don't really want to get into it right now."

Instead, May tells Glue that her parents sent her to boarding school in the UK. Unlike Glue, who cannot return to Canada without a visa, May, though she does not have her HKID with her, has dual citizenship. May says that when she was a student in the UK, she never came back for the holidays. Once a year, her parents would fly to her and the three of them would stay at their home in Sussex.

"Have you seen your parents?" Glue asks.

"Nope."

"What would you say if you saw them?"

A plane lands. Birds start chirping. The polluted water washes up against the rocks. A fisherman walks by.

"I might have seen them once, actually," says May. "It was kind of weird."

"What do you mean?"

"I swear I saw them downstairs once, at the Tsui Wah Restaurant. I saw the two of them eating there. It felt so surreal. Why out of everywhere in Hong Kong they chose to eat at that specific Tsui Wah restaurant? I mean, it's a chain. The one here isn't any better than the other ones.

But they seemed happy. They didn't talk to each other, just held each other's hands and silently walked out when they were done. For a second, I wanted to say something. I imagined that they would be overjoyed to see me and we'd hug, the three of us, right in the middle of the walkway between the MTR station and the restaurant. It would be like a TVB drama. But I didn't. I thought seeing me in Hong Kong would probably give them a heart attack."

Glue does not respond. Maybe Glue is too high. Maybe Glue is thinking about being beaten up by Po-Wing. The two are now searching for a recycling bin, carrying crushed beer cans between their fingers.

"Can I come to yours tonight?" Glue asks.

May nods.

Glue remembers learning that after the Cultural Revolution, there was a short period of time when there were anarchist utopias in two major Chinese cities. Hong Kong was not one of them. In those places, there were no authorities, no police were on the streets; students took turns directing traffic. Maybe living in someone else's apartment, with a borrowed identity, is a similar feeling.

*IT IS* two in the afternoon when Glue wakes up. May is in bed, next to Glue, checking her phone.

Glue sinks back into Rachel Ai-Ming Anderson's parents' king-size bed and wonders, once more, if "May" is May's real name.

"Your headphones," May says. "They're on the nightstand. I found them on the floor last night."

Glue thanks May. "When will we—"

"Want to go for a drive next Sunday? I'll be downstairs at midnight."

Next Sunday is the last Sunday in October. Glue agrees to see May.

"Take your time, Glue." May gets dressed and leaves the apartment, telling Glue that there's somewhere she needs to be and that Glue can stay if he wants. "Help yourself to whatever is in the fridge."

There is beer in the fridge. Glue does not have to work today.

At least one book on everyone's bookshelf will never be read; the one on this bookshelf, Glue thinks, is *Employees First: Inspire, Engage, and Focus on the HEART of Your Organization.* Glue contemplates having a beer. No. Being drunk will not be sufficient. Glue opens the book, *Employees First,* and starts masturbating. Glue cries a little, his tears and cum smeared all over page 58. He returns the book to the shelf and puts his shorts back on before crying some more.

Glue shuts the door to May's apartment. Sometimes, after he ejaculates, his face turns pink, and he begins feeling like a child with a doughnut inside his heart. In such moments, Glue feels that everything he once thought belonged to him was never his in the first place. All he wants, in such moments, is to watch a ten-minute highlight of an NBA game on YouTube and eat noodles. He also wants to fall in love with May, which makes him remember the last time he was in love. It was summer in Toronto. Glue was with Elle; he and Elle were on shrooms. The magic mushrooms made him realize that everything is nothing, and all he had was nothing more than things that his brain made up to remind himself that he existed, and in that moment, in Riverdale Park, on a beige picnic blanket, when it was warm, and the sun was setting, Glue placed his head on Elle's lap. Elle, Glue remembers, who was also on shrooms, looked, at that moment, hopeful. Glue closed his eyes. He imagined that he was dead. This was the afterlife, and the smell of weed and beer and sunscreen emitted from people in small groups surrounding them in the park was the smell of heaven.

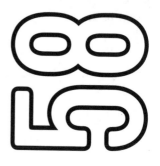

**MORE OFTEN** than not, stories set in Hong Kong end with patricide. Either that or the father figure is completely absent from the story. If neither is the case, then the story, unless it's a state-funded cop show, ends with Hong Kong being completely destroyed. State-funded cop shows end with everyone on a rooftop, in the New Territories, having a barbecue together.

It is the last Sunday in October. May and Glue are meeting for a drive to the New Territories.

May has rented a grey Ferrari Roma. Glue doesn't know that this is the car he is waiting for. He just stares blankly at the slick shiny grey object rumbling in front of him, its tires clean. Glue is reminded of a certain sex toy.

May lowers the window. "What are you doing?" She gestures for Glue to get in.

The roof is too low and the car smells of leather.

"What's with the car?"

May laughs. "It's ridiculous, right? It was the only car they had available for today."

It is midnight. May speeds past all the taxis and trucks on the North Lantau Highway, taking a long way around to get to the New Territories.

Glue, who doesn't have a driver's licence, never thought that he would find himself in a Ferrari. How rich is May? May's job is to develop arguments that problematize institutionalized banking and provide reasons as to why one should start using decentralized currencies. Are crypto firms scams? If so, which is more of a scam: an ESL school or a crypto firm? Sadly, to Glue, a crypto firm seems the more democratic of the two. One of the main arguments for decentralized currencies is that they give people who are unbanked access to funds. But how democratic is that? State power is maintained through violence. All early states are built through colonization and slavery. War, unless it is over natural resources, is used not so much to conquer territory but to conquer populations (cultural assimilation), to (re)concentrate labour (internet for all), and to tax labourers (and digital labourers) for their crops (data).

Except Zomia. Zomia, at the time of this writing, is still made up of non-state spaces. These social spaces—highlands that overlap over ten Asian countries—are occupied by those not of any nation-state. These spaces resist dominant languages. They've even eliminated writing from their cultural practices, to be forgotten, to be free from history.

To May, being able to work remotely, to travel whenever she feels her body needs, is the only way to be free. To Glue, speaking Chinglish to strangers after work is the only way to feel free.

"We're not going to see your parents, right?" Glue needs to make sure.

"Hell, no," May says. "We're just going to drive around for a bit."

The Tsing Ma Bridge is completely empty.

"I have a favour to ask," says Glue. "Can we stop by the cargo terminal on our way back?"

"Sure." May doesn't find this request strange.

From the Ting Kau Bridge, Glue looks back at Tung Chung. Though it only took them fifteen minutes to get here, the lights from the airport, in this smog, look distant.

May lights a cigarette. "Want one?"

"But—"

"I don't care. It's a rental."

*TREES SURROUND* the parking lot. They are the only people at Tai Lam Chung. They park the car and walk towards the main dam. A large stone plate welcomes them.

TAI LAM RESERVOIR
THIS STONE WAS LAID BY HIS EXCELLENCY THE GOVERNOR
SIR ALEXANDER GRANTHAM. G. C. M. G.
ON THE 7TH DAY OF DECEMBER 1957
TO COMMEMORATE THE COMPLETION
OF THE RESERVOIR BEGUN IN 1953

CAPACITY—4500 MILLION GALLONS
HEIGHT OF MAIN DAM—200 FEET

"People come here to have sex, you know?" Glue says.

"What can they do? Land's expensive. You can't fuck next to your parents' room." May cringes. "At least I don't think I can."

The British Empire contributed to the current housing crisis. Hong Kong, colonized, became a trading hub for businesses to access China and the rest of Asia. Everything has value when those with money agree that it does; Hong Kong is the same. Investments come in; housing prices go up. The proximity to neighbouring Asian countries makes Hong Kong doubly expensive. The government doubles down on this; there's no sales tax, making it a great place for tourists and investors.

This is why, sixty-eight years later, Sir Alexander Grantham, when we don't have a place to fuck, we fuck at this dam built to commemorate you.

*SURROUNDED BY* mountains and trees, there's less pollution here. The sky is dark and clear. From the top of the dam, Glue looks down. Two hundred feet below his feet is the reservoir, dark green, lit brightly by towering yellow lights above his head. Glue recalls how May poured water on him after Po-Wing's beating.

May opens an airlock bag with grey wiry strands inside. "Shrooms?"

"Sure."

"In Sweden," May says, "around ten every night, students at this university would open their windows and scream."

"Is this a community-building thing?"

May laughs. "I think they're just stressed."

Glue thinks about screaming. He doesn't. He'll regret not doing it. He'll never come here again.

May gets on the Tuen Mun Road. Residential buildings surround the highway. Glue sees windows of apartment buildings. Lights—blue, yellow, and white—light up this compartmentalized world. The parks are empty. The trams have stopped running. The train tracks are free.

"Music?"

Glue only has a Spotify playlist composed of national anthems. "Sure. Play whatever you want," Glue says.

"Do you know about the 1970 hijacking?" May asks.

Glue doesn't.

"A group of students from elite universities hijacked a Boeing 727," May says. "One was the bass player of this band, Les Rallizes Dénudés. The students wanted to dethrone the Emperor of Japan and threatened the pilots with swords."

*Heavier Than a Death in the Family*[7] is the name of the album May puts on. Glue sees on the infotainment system display that this track is called "The Night Collectors." The airy noise of the electric guitar blasts through Glue's mind. The speakers in the car are comparable to Po-Wing's Bang & Olufsen sound system. Glue has never heard anything of the sort. For a moment, for the first time in his life, he feels as if he understands the music he is listening to—but before his brain can articulate it, the chaotic distortion of sounds

---

7

melts all of his languages into one dirty puddle that the wheels of May's rented Ferrari Roma splash over. A gut-punching pause follows a slight delay of echoes, the foreplay, holding time just long enough for Glue to want more, and then comes a crumbling wall of noise, weighing down Glue's mind, turbulence inside turbulence. Glue feels as if his brain is trying to land on a faraway runway in a matter of seconds. It cracks, reverberates, and squeaks all at once, again and again, submerging and resubmerging Glue's consciousness into a continuous feedback loop. Glue almost vomits.

"The hijackers wanted to fly the plane to Cuba, to join Fidel Castro and learn how to be revolutionaries. But there wasn't enough fuel. They landed in Fukuoka and released the women and children in exchange for more fuel. The plane still couldn't fly that far. So they opted for North Korea, because the Emperor was who they were against, not because they supported Kim Jong-il."

"Where are we going?" Glue can't help but ask. "Are you driving to China? We're awfully close to the border."

Why would May drive to China in the middle of the night in this flashy rental car with someone else's ID?

"They were part of the Japanese Red Army," May says. The music gets louder; May's almost shouting. "Back then, American fighter jets would refuel in Japan before heading to Vietnam. Post-war youths were against it and these students decided to do something about it. But the hijackers didn't land in North Korea. The Japanese, the CIA, and South Korea coordinated a charade."

"A what?"

"Charade." May shuts the windows and lowers the volume. "They tricked them into landing in Seoul. They dressed actors up in Communist uniforms to greet them. The airport was dressed to look like Pyongyang too, with North Korean flags everywhere. They even had a choir, and to make them think they were in North Korean airspace, they had jets fire anti-aircraft shells at the plane before it landed."

"None of them ended up in North Korea?"

"Some of them did, eventually. I think they were forced into becoming spies or something after they got there. They're trapped there still, I think, in North Korea, never made it to Cuba. I kind of lost interest after the South Korea bit. Does it matter what happened after? It's not like what they did changed anything."

May is right. Nothing changed. The American war in Vietnam continued and Japan still has a monarchy. And one important fact remains true: the enemy of your enemy is not your friend. "I think the samurai swords they used might have been fake, too," May adds—an important, albeit uncertain, footnote that should not be edited out.

*THE FERRARI* rushes past power stations and factories and a beach. Why are cities in the world all so similar? Beaches are always so close to power stations. Glue remembers how in Toronto, Sugar Beach is right next to the Redpath Sugar Refinery. Glue recalls an argument he had with Elle at Sugar Beach.

"Your posture."

It was summer. Memories of living with Elle in Toronto are tinted with a shade of brownish yellow, as though looking through the eyes of a mosquito. Elle and Glue were on a patio. It was Glue's idea, to come here on a crowded Sunday afternoon. The two waited for forty-five minutes in the heat before being seated. Elle did not look like she wanted to be there. Two tall Goose Island IPAs stood in front of them. "Do you mind sitting straight?" Elle asked Glue, who was staring blankly at the people on the beach. This was towards the end of their relationship.

"Like what?" Glue tried his best to keep his voice neutral.

"I know you think being fixated on table manners and posture is classist," Elle said, "but no one else sits like you do. My parents would have sent me away from the dinner table if I sat like you."

Glue attempted to adjust his posture. When he tried to emulate Elle's posture, he felt awkward. "You're making me anxious. Now I don't know how to sit," Glue said.

Elle rolled her eyes and chugged some beer. "You're also making that face again."

"What face?"

"That you're all innocent and that I'm bullying you."

It was Glue's turn to roll his eyes. In this uncomfortable silence on a hot afternoon, they finished their beers.

"This is suffocating," Elle said.

When the waiter came over to ask if the two wanted anything else, Elle said no before Glue could say anything. When the bill came, Glue paid.

With May, Glue never feels pressured to pay. With Elle, Glue always felt responsible for the bill. Glue felt as though it was because of him that Elle moved in after Gwen left Toronto, and because Elle moved into his apartment, into his life in Toronto, he was responsible for her. Elle, who was brought up in a wealthy family, who'd had an Amex card since she was a teen, who spent much of her adult life with friends who attended the same private high school as her, friends who would take turns paying for the entire table when they went out, never thought about whose responsibility it was to pay the bill. To Elle—and Glue knew this well—if the day came when she asked Glue to split the bill with her, it would be the day the two of them were no longer romantically involved. This seemed normal to Glue at the time.

After all, debt is a form of social exchange, and social exchanges are how human relationships are maintained.

Nothing changes. May told Glue that something of his was stolen and Glue took *Employees F1rst* from the bookshelf and cried and ejaculated into it. Glue feels that his relationship with May is a good one.

**MAY'S FERRARI** speeds past yet another beach and two more power stations, a farm, and a fishing wharf. Now they're on Deep Bay Road. Glue checks his phone and the only identifiable stop on Google Maps in their proximity is a location called Chung Pak Nai Public Toilet No. 1. It has three stars on Google Maps.

May stops the car on top of Lau Fau Shan. Below them is Shenzhen Bay. Though only a short drive away, the water here is much more contaminated than that of the reservoir.

"Glue," May says. "Do you trust me?"

Glue hesitates. "I don't know, May."

"If I tell you to get out of the car," May says, "would you trust that I will come back to get you?"

Glue starts laughing. "What?"

May avoids eye contact with Glue.

Glue shakes his head, still smiling, and steps out of the vehicle.

May drives away.

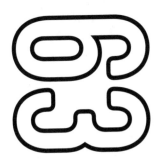

*STARING AT* Shenzhen Bay, Glue takes out his dick and tries to take a piss, but nothing comes out. It is probably best that he doesn't piss right now. Glue imagines a scenario where a government official comes and collects Glue's urine sample. They would certainly find substances that are illegal in his piss. The thought makes Glue laugh. When he stops laughing, he realizes that the Ferrari is nowhere in sight. He is alone. This makes him laugh some more. He thinks about the time when Elle complained about his posture. Though this memory upsets Glue, he knows that Elle is right. His back does ache sometimes and he does, indeed, have bad posture. Then why was he so mad? Glue puts his dick away. He will piss later. He sits down on a rock and starts crying. He feels as though his heart is being cleansed as tears fall from his eyes onto the soil. This makes him smile.

May is back. She honks. Glue tries to wipe away his tears before turning around.

"Sorry," May says. "We're good. I just needed to drive around alone for a bit."

Glue is not mad at all. Instead, he completely understands.

"Have you been crying?" asks May.

Glue, instead of answering, asks May for some hand sanitizer. After he disinfects his hands, he tries to kiss May, who pushes him away, a soft push.

"Later," says May.

*THE BRIDGE* that leads to the mainland is bright and yellow. Across the sea, amidst the fog, Glue can see Shenzhen's towers shooting red lights into the sky. During the day, bamboo rafts can be seen, rising up and down with the waves between Hong Kong and Shenzhen. When Hong Kong became modernized (Westernized), it also became a filter. This assimilated place is how mainland China benefited from free-market capitalism while keeping Westernization at a distance (Hong Kong being the distance). Where Glue and May are is one of the points where this distance ends.

Everything is nothing. The psychedelic experimental rock music continues playing. What, Glue now wonders, was he trying so frantically to defend since he returned from Canada? Absolutely nothing. Nil. This might be a terrifying reckoning, but Glue, through the windshield of the Italian sports car, watching the polluted sky absorb the light from Shenzhen's skyscrapers, in this comfort, which is peace, remains calm as ever. Everything is okay. Maybe Glue knew this all along. In fact, everything is going according to plan. Algorithms control the future controls the present. Glue is simply fulfilling prophecy. Po-Wing was right. Glue is a privileged chink who attended an international school—the most elitist, most bureaucratic, most colonial of all institutions—and, to top it off, he received a Western post-secondary education, without governmental support. He dropped out of graduate school, which was good because he drifted back to where he is supposed to be—here, teaching English to those who aspire to assimilate. The cause is the consequence. Three years before the handover, he was born. This was called British Hong Kong. His entire raison d'être, from the moment of his birth, has been colonized. He cannot even type in traditional Chinese without using the romanized input method—Pinyin. This is great. 天生我材必有用—李白 (All things in their being are good for something—Li Bai). Now, twenty-six years later, what is there left for him to do but accept his role in society? He is part of the orchestra. He is an ESL instructor for Englishmentation. In his next stage of life, Glue won't need to prepare for classes. All he needs to do, from now on, is simply turn off his mind. He will correct pronunciation mistakes and assign marks to students' standardized tests mechanically. Accepting this fact is freedom. Maybe he should even get in touch with Lester Tse—might as well help him out at his immigration consultancy firm and earn some extra cash. He is prepared for that job, assisting people who want to assimilate, assimilate to Western society. All of this is what Glue is meant to do. We're now twenty-four years into the fifty-year plan. Everything here is perfect.

The rumbling sounds from Les Rallizes Dénudés are unhinged; it's as if the recording itself was dipped in acid. The melody struggles to rise on top. Chaos drowns it—the delayed kick of the drum and the off-beat hitting of the snare. This is the sound of Glue's silent dreams. Glue holds his breath. This is what it sounds like—the dark sea with a thousand waves and no earth. Glue's dreams were visualizations of these songs he has never heard, these outlandish mixtures of sounds. And then everything evaporates. All at once, all comes to an abrupt end. Even the echoes cut off. May's phone runs out of battery and Glue, in this instance, realizes that he no longer cares about what May stole.

**ALL**, for a second, becomes sober. A chill rushes through Glue's body. His neck is goose-pimpled; he lets out a shiver. For a second, Glue thinks about Elle.

"You want to play something else?"

Glue shakes his head.

May turns off the air con, lowers the windows. They smell the pollution. The wind is warm. Their skin, cool from the air-conditioned car a moment ago, becomes greasy from the sudden humidity and dust.

"Why did you want to drive here?" Glue asks. Glue assumes that May has an attachment to this area. Perhaps her parents brought her here when she was younger. Or a former lover did.

"I heard it's nice," May says simply.

Glue doesn't press any further. The rules they have between them allow conversations to come to abrupt stops. Geographically speaking, it is also fitting that they are speaking to each other where Hong Kong ends. Here, they let their questions hang indefinitely in the air.

"Remember I stole something of yours?" May asks.

"No," Glue answers. For a moment, Glue almost wants to tell May that he ejaculated in a book of hers and that things are even. But he doesn't feel the need to anymore. Perhaps this is how revenge works.

May smiles. "Do you still want to go to the cargo terminal?"

Glue shakes his head. "You're going to leave soon, aren't you?"

"Ask something else."

"Is 'May' your real name?"

"No," May answers swiftly. "Tell me a childhood memory."

This is the first memory that comes to Glue's mind: Glue is doing groceries with his father. Owners at the wet markets, knowing customers will haggle, raise their prices a little at first. Glue's father never asks for a lower price. He just pays whatever they ask for. The owners look at Glue's father as though he is a bourgeois fool. Some even lower the price for his father since he accepts without hesitation.

May doesn't comment on Glue's story. She does not share a childhood memory of her own, either. Instead, she says, "When I was a teen, I wanted to make a game."

"Like a video game?" Glue asks.

"Like a video game, set in a world exactly like this one. The player is thrown into an identity, a person living in this world. The score goes down the longer the character is alive. The goal of the game is to remove yourself from the world as quickly and as discreetly as possible, without leaving any traces behind."

"I'll remember driving around with you," says Glue. He asks May if it would be okay if he takes a piss. He takes May's small bottle of hand sanitizer with him and a pack of tissue.

Overlooking the Shenzhen Bay, Glue urinates in a bush.

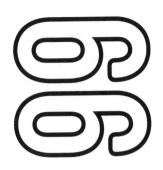

忍

This Chinese character can mean "restrain," "tolerate," "endure," "bear," and "forbearance," but it can also mean "invisible," "cruel," or even "too tragic to look at." Fanon wrote that "the cause is the consequence" (*The Wretched of the Earth*). Is it right that we compare colonial pasts to parenting? Film scholars argue that these narrative tropes in Hong Kong films, missing father figures, ending with patricide, and/or the complete destruction of Hong Kong, present a straightforward critique of China. Then, is Great Britain the mom? That hundred-year-old racist cunt.

# NOSTALGIA

# ARE

# LIES

**"LET'S READ** the following exchange out loud," says Glue. "I will play Emily and you can read Aiden's. Okay, Kazuo?"

"Okay."

EMILY: How is your family?
AIDEN: They're good. Mom's always in the kitchen, she practically lives there.
EMILY: Haha. She must cook a lot. What is your favourite dish?
AIDEN: Hmm, chicken-fried steak. I basically like fried food.
EMILY: Oh. I hear you. I love that, too. How is your dad?
AIDEN: He's good. My dad is a man of wisdom. I can discuss everything with him.
EMILY: That's great. He must be experienced.

"Okay, great, Kazuo. Now, repeat after me. We do not have to volunteer at the firm. Pay attention to the *v*," Glue says. "It's pronounced 'vä'—välunteer."

"Volunteer."

"Good, Kazuo. Then why are you going to the firm today?"

"Because it good to have more experience at the firm."

"Good, Kazuo. Good. You're doing a fantastic job. To end the lesson, let's practise saying this phrase. Are you ready, Kazuo?"

"Yes, sir."

"Snow is white is true."

"Snow is white is true."

"If and only if snow is white."

"If and only is snow is white."

"Great, Kazuo. Let's say it again faster," Glue says.

"Snow is white is true if and only if snow is white."

"Faster."

"Snow is white is true if and only if snow is white."

"Faster."

"Snowiswhiteistrueifandonlyifsnowiswhite."

"Again."

"Snowiswhiteistrueifandonlyifsnowiswhite. Snowiswhite-istrueifandonlyifsnowiswhite. Snowiswhiteistrueifandonly-ifsnowiswhite."

"Stop! Excellent job, Kazuo. See you tomorrow!"

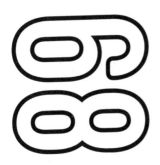

"*D UP*, boi!"

"I know *lah, diu*," Glue says. "This one. The skinny. He can't shoot. I just back off."

The high-schooler misses a three.

Glue grabs the rebound, passes the ball to his teammate. "*Diu*, I knew he can't shoot *lah*."

The high-schooler, in his yellow-and-blue gym uniform, with dry acned skin, remains silent on defence as Glue tries to post him up on the block. "Mismatch here, *ah*! I take him. I take him."

It's too hot. Glue's Filipino teammates do not have the stamina to question this Kong dude's accent. They pass him the ball in the post so that he'll shut up. Glue spins past the high-schooler and tries to lay the ball in reverse. He has done this move countless times, since he himself was in high school, taking off on one foot and completing a reverse layup with ease. But his back is stiff from long hours of sitting. Elle is right. Glue's posture sucks. He also drinks too much. Glue doesn't have the strength to extend his arm and release the ball on the other side of the rim. He takes an extra step. The ball goes in.

"走步!" (*Travel!*) Except the high-schooler doesn't remember how to say it in English. Apart from Glue there are no Chinese people in this game. Glue, because he spent his entire day teaching ESL, needs the two points he just scored to count to restore his self-esteem.

Glue ignores this scrawny chink and tries to post him up again on the next play. "Yo. One more, ah. One more, ah. This the mismatch. Mouse in da house here. Feed me. Feed me."

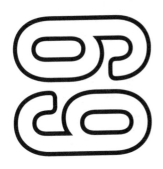

*"CAN I SPEAK* the Chinglish?"

"What is up with you?"

Glue can feel Gwen frowning over the phone. "Chinglish more comfortable, *ah mah*."

"Lester's business is doing well," Gwen says. "He needs more help, wants you to help him out if you have time."

"Why you do the calling. Everybody texting, not call, using the WhatsApp, the WeChat, the whatnot. You, only you do the calling me. No one else calls me."

"What are you up to on the weekends these days?"

Apparently Gwen has no interest in discussing why she's calling.

"Sometimes I do the IELTS grading."

"Would you rather help Lester?"

"What I do, ah?"

"Ask him yourself if you're interested."

"*Diu.* Why he not the one asking me. He do himself the asking, *ah mah. Ding.* If he want me help him."

"What are you saying?"

"Why he want my help he don't do the asking me him-self ah, that Lester Tse . . . *Diu*. Tell him do the asking *lah*."

"*Diu!* 講中文就講中文啦!" (If you're gonna speak to me in Canto, speak Canto!)

Glue swiftly changes the subject. "We're seeing Mom and Dad this weekend, right?"

"Yeah. I'll come pick you up at nine."

**GLUE CLIMBS** into the passenger seat of Gwen's SUV. "Where's Lester Tse?" Glue's eye sockets are droopy, his facial hair is unkempt, and his glasses are sliding to the tip of his oily nose.

"Why is your shirt so wrinkly?"

"*Aya*. My iron broke. Doesn't matter *lah*, just yum cha, just in the car. No one gives the fuck *lah*. Immigration officers will not let me in 'cause my shirt wrinkly, meh? I don't think so. Those middle-age man wearing the Rolex going to do that gambling-gambling all day all wear the wrinkly shirt *lah*. It's Macau ah, Gwen Wu—"

"Okay. Shut up. You don't own a watch and Lester's going to meet us there."

"Why new car?"

"He needs to drive around to meet clients these days, so we decided to get another car. He got this one for me. What do you think?"

"*Wa*. Lucky you *lah*, Gwen Wu. You have the big SUV now. So loaded. Like the rich Karen—"

"Stop saying random shit."

There's a moment of silence. It has only been a few minutes that the two have been in the car together, but Gwen looks like she needs a break. Gwen sighs. "Did you talk to him yet?"

"The Lester?"

"Yes." Gwen makes a right turn and takes a sip from her Starbucks paper cup. "Your accent sounds way too self-aware and confident to be that of a Kong dude."

Glue decides to ignore Gwen's remark. "Yes ah. I told the Lester *lah*. I help if he need, on the weekend and evenings for now. I told him I do less of the IELTS grading. He want me to tell the client how good the Canada is *wo*. The air is nice. The food is cheaper than Hong Kong. *Diu*. To be honest, everywhere a little cheaper than Hong Kong *lah*. Canada not Dubai. He said to say to the people Canada safer, too. No gun. Not America. Not England. We don't have the Boris Johnson. *Diu*. But I know some people here like the Boris Johnson. Da fuck I supposed to do? Some Kong dudes like the Trump even. I think everything he doing a bit dishonest *lor*. To be honest. Compare the Canada to the America of course a little safer *lah, diu*."

They have both heard, though they haven't talked about it, that there are increasing reports of Anti-Asian violence in the West.

"It's their choice to leave, Glue. You're just there to help them do what they want to do."

"But what if what they get is not—"

"Glue. If you don't like it, don't work for Lester. I don't feel like talking about this anymore."

"Sorry *lor*. So angry these days. That coffee for me?"

Gwen stares ahead at the road.

"Thank you, Gwen."

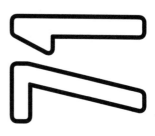

*IT IS* the middle of November. Though it is sometimes hot still, the air conditioning is no longer turned on. The dry air cuts Glue's unmoisturized skin, leaving a layer of white dust.

"A lot of our clients are older," whispers Lester Tse. "Like your parents." Lester Tse takes a sip of tea.

Glue looks at his mom and his dad. His mother's hair is greyer than he remembers from back in July. His father seems to have gained some weight, and the same large metal-framed glasses that have been resting on his nose from the time Glue was born somehow seem heavier.

"They want to leave, don't want to live the rest of their lives in Hong Kong—but they can't keep up anymore and just want someone telling them where to go and how to live. They don't really care where, as long as it's safe. You can keep doing the Chinglish thing, too. Your sister told me that makes you feel more comfortable, yeah? My clients, hearing that you, having lived in Canada, still speak broken

English, will feel much more comfortable moving there. Speak to me with that accent in front of them, okay?" Lester Tse says this politely; being able to disguise the condescension in each of his words is a gift. Whenever they meet, Lester Tse approaches Glue from behind and massages his shoulders as he greets everyone else at the table, which is how he entered the scene earlier, right when all the food arrived. Lester Tse is always fashionably late. Lester Tse's sleeves are rolled up and his skinny knit tie is nonchalantly tucked in between the buttons of his tight, perfectly ironed white dress shirt.

"You two should eat while it's hot," says Glue's mom. Glue's parents are in a good mood, overjoyed that their son has a stable job as an ESL teacher and that their son and their soon-to-be son-in-law will be working together.

Glue's dad says, "I know you three are busy these days. Don't feel you need to come to Macau every few months anymore."

Glue nods, chewing his chicken feet.

"I'm never too busy for dim sum," says Lester Tse.

"Look at Glen Wu." Glue's mom says this as Glue pours everyone tea, chewing all the while. "He looks so tired. Must be so busy teaching all day."

Glue nods again. Gwen, perhaps annoyed at Glue's silence and his ugly sucking of the chicken feet, and at his wrinkly polo shirt, slaps Glue in the back of his head. The tip of Glue's nose gently grazes the surface of his red tea.

"Hey! No fights," says their dad.

"Gross," Gwen whispers to Glue. "No wonder you haven't seen anyone seriously for so long."

Glue keeps sucking on his steamed chicken feet. His eyes are sleepy, and his unkempt facial hair quivers as he tongues the taste out from each of the bones.

"Glen Wu!" Glue's mom shakes her head. "I know you're busy but maybe you should go to the salon. Get a shave, you know, maybe a haircut, too. I'll pay for you. I know someone here. They're quite good."

"It's okay, Mom," Gwen says. "I booked him an appointment already—a salon in Causeway, for tomorrow." Neither of them has ever gotten a good haircut in Macau.

**LESTER HAS** some meetings, so he leaves early. Gwen and Glue drive back to Hong Kong. Nothing ever changes. Once again they find themselves alone on the world's longest open-sea fixed link—the Hong Kong–Zhuhai–Macao Bridge—where there is only fog and dark green sea. The sky is bright and grey, and if a Hollywood director sees this scene, they will certainly have monsters fight here. It will be the climax of the movie. The bridge will, of course, be destroyed. Maybe if the monsters are big enough, they'll use the bridge as a weapon. The end of the bridge disappears into the distance. The polluted sky and the polluted sea become one. Glue feels as if at any given moment, the world will swallow this SUV and no one will know that these siblings ever existed.

"*Wa.* So scary out here," says Glue. "Terrifying to drive home alone here *wo.*"

"Lester does it all the time."

"The Lester Tse, I wonder, does he ever cry?"

"What?"

"You seen the Lester Tse cry before?"

Gwen has to think. "No."

Glue thinks about Po-Wing. There are some people who never cry.

They hear the wind. There's no radio out here.

"Want da beer? You should come up for a bit."

"I have to drive home, Glue."

"What you have planned this afternoon?"

"I'm going to go for a swim."

"Oh yes. Of course. You have da indoor swimming pool in your building now. So nice."

Gwen ignores Glue's comment.

"Do you mind parking in the garage? Come up for a bit. I need your help to throw out the mattress."

Gwen rolls her eyes. Glue thinks that because that was the first grammatically correct sentence he uttered all day, Gwen finds his request, though clingy, to be sincere. "Fine. But I'm going to book an appointment for you, at the salon in Causeway, and you're going tomorrow."

The curtains in Gwen's old room, once white, are becoming yellow, and the wooden floor is sticky from the humidity. The two of them leave their masks on to lift the dust-covered mattress up.

"This is going to ruin my clothes," says Gwen.

"That's why you should dress like me, with the shit polo shirt."

"Ugh. Do we need to do this today? Let's just leave it here. It's not like you're going to use this room, right?"

"You sure?" Glue is surprised. Gwen never procrastinates.

"I'm tired. I'll take the beer."

Glue has Tsing Tao in the fridge. Gwen takes off her socks, folds her legs, and chugs half of the light yellow beer from the green bottle.

"*Wa*. Sister. Calm down *lah*. Why drink so fast?"

"It's fucking stuffy in here. Give me a break. Did you clean the air con? Why is it so loud and why is it taking so long for cold air to come out?"

"Oh. Sor."

Gwen shakes her head and starts checking her phone. "Are you actually down to work with Lester?" Gwen scrolls through Twitter.

Glue is on a stool, his face up against the air conditioner. He gives it a gentle slap. The air con rumbles a wet rumble and spits out some cool air. "Don't want to talk about da work *ah diu*." The truth is, Glue thinks that he would not mind the job that much. Though he thinks the job is, in essence, the same as teaching ESL, he has a feeling, deep inside, that one day he will become an immigration consultant. "Can I ask you da fava?"

"What now?"

"Can you watch da episode of National Geographic documentary wif me before you go?"

Gwen frowns. "Why are you so strange?" But she agrees. She doesn't drink often. After finishing this beer, she should probably wait for a bit before she drives.

Glue smiles, turns on the TV, and starts playing the National Geographic show about scammers.

How is it a scam when the person you are scamming is part of the reason why you need to scam people for a living? Throughout the show, Gwen, maybe because she's drinking, begins to complain, saying that what's right and what's wrong are decided by countries with money and power. She tells Glue that the privatization of knowledge, the idea of intellectual property, copyright infringement, the very idea of originality, differs from culture to culture. "Is copying, coming up with ways, outside of the 'rules,' to make a living, immoral? If so, why? Who is this TV host to 'expose' people who resort to selling counterfeit goods for a living?" Glue recalls the many whitewashed Hollywood remakes of films from other countries. "Western media, especially Hollywood, steals ideas and makes them their own. They end up making everything so didactic."

Gwen nods, takes a sip of beer, her eyes fixated on the screen. "At least counterfeit goods, copies of copies, don't concern themselves with being the original. The very idea of originality is completely undermined. They're all just copies." Gwen's voice gets louder. "Plus, it's not like the vendors are making a fuckload of money selling counterfeit goods."

Glue tries to interject but Gwen is not done.

"And who even is this self-righteous motherfucker,

coming here to 'get scammed'? Why doesn't he go 'expose' the triads behind these scams then?" Gwen is saying this, not so much to Glue, but to herself. Gwen googles the name of the host. Conor Woodman—a television host who was married to Phoebe Waller-Bridge. Woodman wrote a book—*Unfair Trade: The Shocking Truth Behind "Ethical" Business.*

Gwen says, "This reminds me of when we were at that climate protest with Elle."

Glue nods. It was a Saturday. Elle and Gwen busted into Glue's room, dragged him out of bed and downstairs to join the protestors who were walking down Bay Street. Glue, who cared about environmental issues but was hungover, was reluctant to join. But Elle and Gwen started banging on pans and woks with their spatulas. Protestors were advocating for the Canadian government to adopt a more significant level of greenhouse gas control by 2030, instead of the proposed 2050. A couple years later, all of them left Canada and did not follow up on the news. Maybe Elle did.

"You know how Elle's doing?"

"No," says Glue. "She hasn't been returning my calls."

Gwen continues complaining. Glue can tell that Gwen is trying to change the topic. Perhaps drinking the Tsing Tao was a good idea; Gwen, criticizing the TV show, is getting worked up. Glue has not seen Gwen like this in a long while.

Glue wonders why Lester Tse, of all people, is who Gwen decides to be with. Glue doesn't ask her this.

"You have a lint roller?" Gwen asks, when the episode

is over. Gwen says she can stay a little longer, but, since they're just watching television, she might as well clean off the dust on her blouse and light blue ripped jeans.

Glue thinks about asking if Gwen would like to have pizza together tonight. There's a Pizza Hut that makes mediocre and overpriced pizza downstairs. It will only take twenty minutes for them to get a fresh pizza delivered. But he doesn't ask Gwen. Glue should let her go home.

**LESTER TSE'S** immigration consultancy's office is the lofty kind in an old factory building in Kowloon Bay. The large elevators were designed to transport goods. Nothing ever changes. The office is a few stops away from Diamond Hill station. Glue is now taking the same route to work as he did back when he attended the Queen's Music Academy. Lester's firm shares the floor with a startup company. Sometimes, the tech bros who work half days on Saturdays play ping-pong in the office across the hall.

"So, Mr. Tam." Glue, having commuted here from Tung Chung, having spent an hour and fifteen minutes on the MTR, switching trains three times and drinking three cans of iced coffee from 7-Eleven, is less hungover than he otherwise would be. He also shaved, but his Uniqlo U polo shirt, which he got on sale, remains wrinkly. "After reviewing your résumé, savings, and educational background, I suggest that you move to Calgary. There is a large Chinese community there. Many from Hong Kong moved there in the eighties. It's a short flight to Vancouver. Taxes are lower there, too."

"Isn't it cold there?"

"Yes, but so is everywhere else in Canada, Mr. Tam."

"And dry?"

"I know a great brand. They make the best humidifiers. We can discuss the finer details later. I see that you worked at a law firm for eight years, Mr. Tam, as an accountant. I suggest that once you move, you open your own business. With your savings, you will be able to franchise a convenience store. Maybe an INS Market. You'd be creating jobs that way, increasing your chances of getting permanent residency."

"A convenience store? How does that relate to what I do?"

"I understand, Mr. Tam. But this is the easiest way for you to migrate. The province needs jobs. You'd be your own boss, and you'd be creating jobs for others."

"Is franchising a business the only option? Why can't I—"

"It's not, Mr. Tam." Glue lowers his voice, for dramatic effect. "Vivian Li referred you to us, didn't she?"

"Yes."

"So, I guess there's no point in going through all the formalities. No more, as they say"—Glue switches to his Chinglish—"beating around da bush." An inside joke about himself for himself.

Mr. Tam frowns.

Glue coughs, trying not to laugh at the absurdity of this moment. "Do you have the $250,000 Canadian saved up?" Glue asks.

Mr. Tam nods.

"We have connections to a private Chinese business there. They can issue you a job offer for a management position and apply for a visa on your behalf. They'll pretend to have you as an employee for two years, during which you can apply for permanent residency. If not, you can continue paying them to pay you. They will also give you a reference letter for a new job once you 'quit.'"

"How will that work?"

"You'll give us the $250,000. We'll split $50,000 with them, and they will give you back the rest over the course of two years, in the form of a salary. You have to pay tax, of course."

"I have that much. But that's all I have. When I asked Vivian, she told me it was a little cheaper than that. So I thought—"

"Mr. Tam. I see that you attended university in the UK?"

Mr. Tam nods.

"It must have been expensive, especially back then. Your parents supported you, I assume?"

Mr. Tam looks away, looking almost embarrassed.

Glue notices Mr. Tam's watch—TAG Heuer. "You do have some money saved up, but I . . ." Glue pauses. "If I can be honest, I know Vivian wouldn't be recommending you if your family didn't have your back. My boss, Lester Tse—again, for your sake, Mr. Tam, I'm just being honest—Lester Tse is very selective about whom he takes on as clients."

"I know. I know." Mr. Tam, though he sounds hesitant, also seems grateful to be a part of Lester Tse's exclusive group of clients.

"Think of it this way—your parents' money is just your money in the future. Don't be afraid to use it."

Mr. Tam sighs.

"Mr. Tam. You have a daughter, too, correct?"

Mr. Tam nods.

"When I first came back from Canada, I thought I wanted to be a drama teacher. But, of course, teachers in Hong Kong are overworked and don't get paid much because they get to do something 'meaningful.' But money goes to people who go to where the money is. Nothing has anything to do with 'meaning.' So I pivoted. Unlike many of my peers, I took what the market needed." Glue learned this from Netflix, some K-drama about startups—when your client is unconvinced, tell them something vaguely personal. It doesn't even have to relate directly to what is being discussed.

"What does that have to do with my daughter?"

"How old is Sandy this year?"

"She's turning thirteen."

"Middle school, then."

"What's that?"

"She'll be attending middle school in Canada, equivalent to year two of secondary school here. Now, if you don't mind, Mr. Tam, could you tell me which school Sandy attends?"

"Kowloon Tong School."

"Not bad."

Mr. Tam nods proudly. "Yeah. I think she has potential."

"Still a public school, though."

"I'm sorry?"

"Are you a chauvinist, Mr. Tam? Or a Nationalist?"

"Obviously not! What makes you ask that?"

"Sandy will be entering her formative years. Do you really want her to be learning censored material in her classes? Or would you rather Sandy study somewhere where critical thinking is valued?"

Mr. Tam looks down, as if to confront the fact that what Glue is saying is true, and that he has known all along that, for his daughter's sake, he would need to move away from Hong Kong.

Glue feels as if he's bullying Mr. Tam. This moment feels necrophilic. But Glue is now mature. He is no longer a grad student teaching at Atlantia Education. He doesn't feel guilty when he says, "International school will cost you around three hundred thousand Hong Kong dollars a year, Michael. Sorry—may I call you Michael?"

"Sure."

Michael probably does have access to his family's money, but perhaps he does not have a great relationship with his parents, and has never asked for funds to send Sandy to a private school. Perhaps being a single father has also made it difficult. "Sending Sandy to an international school will cost a little more than a third of your current salary, Michael. You have a mortgage, too. You can sell your place, which will be more than enough for a townhouse in Calgary. Sandy can go to public school. It'll be free, too. We both grew up in the nineties, Mr. Tam. If I'm being honest, we both know Hong Kong is not what it was back in the good old days. We were free. We were safe. Now, we're not even protected by the law. The state and law enforcement are here to control us. I'm sure you know what I mean, Michael. Live in Calgary for now. You can move elsewhere later, after obtaining your permanent residency. I promise, your daughter will have a better life in the West."

"But—"

"Michael. Do you remember the incident where the central government cancelled the exam question that asked students, 'What are the pros and cons of Japan's colonization of Hong Kong?' When they ended up deciding that marks would not count for those who chose to answer that question?"

"Sure."

"I'm speaking to you as a former educator right now. I am, as they say, 'putting on da teacher's hat.' Japan made Hong Kong much more civilized than it otherwise would have been. It is the history of colonialism and trade that makes us unique. If we can't think critically about questions like these, about the good things other countries have brought us, how can we have a better future? Here, you can't even protest safely anymore."

"Is that not the case in Canada?"

Glue remembers reading about the Critical Infrastructure Defence Act—one also cannot protest safely against the building of pipelines in Alberta. Democracy, after all, is nothing but the legitimization of conquered land, not the promise of freedom. "In Canada," Glue tries to pivot, "you can criticize the central government and the CCP all you want, but what's the point? Once you get there, you two will have better things to worry about."

"*GOOD JOB*, Glue." Lester Tse pats Glue's shoulder as he walks away.

When Glue returns home from Lester Tse's office, he sees an email from a former graduate school professor of his. Glue is invited to participate in a writing project concerning the dialogical relations between pedagogy, performance art, and ecology. Ecology? Why is Glue invited to do this? The email invites Glue, along with other contributors, to each write 150 words by the end of the month. Is this email intended for him? Sure, he attended teachers' college and has a background in drama—but he dropped out of the writing program after one semester, and he doesn't even recall ever participating in this professor's course.

Glue doesn't respond to the email. The deadline to submit passes.

*GLUE*, though he doesn't remember if he ate anything the previous night, knows that he drank. He passes out during one of his lessons. He has multiple tabs open on the computer screen: Facebook, Instagram, Twitter, Reddit, Weibo, Tencent Video, and Pornhub. He also has a YouTube video open. Lee Sedol, the best Go player on earth, is defeated by Google's AlphaGo. "I failed," reads the closed captioning. Was it gin that he put in his coffee this morning? Regardless, Glue drank it on an empty stomach. He passes out and misses all his appointments at Englishmentation.

Glue wakes up, looks at the screen, and replays the video—might as well finish watching it.

For the rest of the week, he repeats his routine. He wakes up and downs the whiskey next to his bed before breakfast. He almost passes out during his lessons. One time, he vomits into a trash can under the desk and tells the student that the lesson will have to end early.

Another time, Glue accidentally shares his screen

with his student while three of the eight tabs he has open are porn.

"Teacher Wu. If you miss any more of your appointments, we will have to reduce your hours."

"I understand." Glue might be drunk still.

"We, as a school—"

"Company."

"I'm sorry, Teacher Wu?"

"Nothing."

"At this school, we require our instructors to maintain a level of professionalism."

Glue misses several more lessons the following week.

It is a Thursday. It is the end of November. Glue wakes up. His breath stinks of whiskey. His hair—unkempt—is still wet from when he took a shower last night. It now resembles a bird's nest. He finds that he can no longer log in to his Englishmentation teacher's account. He receives an email, telling him that his final paycheque will be made out to him soon.

**GLUE TELLS** Gwen that he was fired from his ESL job. Gwen knows that Glue is reluctant to work for Lester Tse full-time, Glue can tell, which is why Gwen does not mention Lester. Instead she tells Glue that she will reach out to her former boss at the private school in Shenzhen.

"A new position just opened up in Shenzhen," Gwen tells Glue a week later. Glue reaches out to the school and is invited for a second interview.

"What would you do in such a situation?" the manager asks. He is wearing the same pale pink shirt, no blazer this time. This is their second meeting. His sleeves are rolled up, showing his new Rolex, which at some point in the conversation he will stare at, for a moment, in a satisfying way. His shirt is tucked into his navy blue slacks. Perhaps he decided to lose the blazer because he is in better shape. He also dyed his hair brown. He has a new belt too, this one from Hermès. Glue, to his own amazement, finds him quite handsome this time.

"Well, I would try my best to not confront the student directly but have a dialogue with the entire class about race."

"Remember, Glen. This needs to be done carefully."

"I will tell the class why we need to respect each other's cultures and that to maintain a safe and welcoming learning environment, any language of such kind should not be allowed."

"Is there anything else you would like to add?"

"I might also reference social movements about racial inequality happening around the world." Glue thinks for a bit. "Without being specific. I will add that many people in the world at this moment are fighting for equality."

"What if a student asks you to provide an example?"

"Well—"

"This is my advice for you, Glen. Given that you are referred here by Gwen, I'm going to let you through to the next round, but when you encounter such a situation when you are teaching your demo class, situations about race or other sensitive social issues, it would be best if you have the students look information up themselves without referring specifically to which side you think is right or what movement you support."

"Got it. Thank you for your advice."

"Last year, we had some issues. Some of the parents here are not the most open-minded people, you know. So a lot of the social problems, we avoid addressing directly. We want students to be informed but try to do this while maintaining a good image in front of the parents. Also—" he continues before Glue can respond, "some of the social issues happening in the West, they might not have much to do with our students here, you know?"

"What do you mean?"

"Students here, they don't need to fight what the minorities in the West fight. Here, it's much safer, much more peaceful."

"I'm just wondering—"

"Yes?"

"How can we teach students how social movements work with such a mindset if we've already decided that it's not their responsibility to care about what others elsewhere are fighting for? And I don't necessarily think that what happens elsewhere has no relation to our students here."

The manager takes a sip of water. "Since I have decided to move your application forward, Glen, I'm wondering if I could ask you a question. This is off the record, between the two of us."

"Sure." Glue feels like there's no way he could say no.

"I never thought I'd enjoy working here but I really do. Here, there is a clear line between what we are allowed to say and what we are not. There's none of that talk about free speech and cancel culture. In Hong Kong, we are testing that line still, so we're not too good at it." He notices Glue frowning. "I'm sorry, am I making you uncomfortable?"

Glue shakes his head.

"Glen, the interview is over. Go ahead and ask whatever questions you might have."

"Earlier, you mentioned that the social movements that happen elsewhere have nothing to do with our students here. I'm just wondering what you mean by that."

"Well, since we're off the record—" He gives Glue a smile. "Some of the things I say might sound bad out of context. Previously, I had some trouble with teachers talking about Black Lives Matter. The whole matter was presented without nuance."

"Without nuance?"

"They told the students that minority-on-minority crime is a result of white supremacy. I had some problems with that. You can't be telling me that the reason Chinese people hate Japanese people and Japanese people hate Koreans is because of white people. Plus, many white people, white women especially, are victims of police violence as well. So trying not to speak on such issues is simply a preventive measure . . . we're taking."

Glue will never hear back about the job.

*IF THE* driver asks Glue where he is from, Glue will tell him that he is Japanese. The driver doesn't ask Glue where he is from.

Glue texts Gwen. It is time to be honest. Glue tells her that he feels like shit. Glue also tells Gwen that before the interview, he sent some single parent to Calgary and convinced him to sell his apartment in Hong Kong. Gwen tells Glue that *If moving is what they think they want, then the least you can do as their immigration consultant is to help them.* She also tells Glue that everyone from a former colony should have the right to move wherever they want. Glue agrees but knows that right now, it is only the rich who can move. Gwen, of course, should be fully aware of this. Glue doesn't text this thought to Gwen.

Glue, instead, texts May, asks if she wants to go out for drinks.

*Sorry, can't right now. I'm out.*

*Out where?*

*Ask something else.*

*Why are you out?*

May replies thirty minutes later.

May sends a picture of an egg tart, resting in her palm. The surface of the tart is glazed with a thin layer of brown sugar. Glue is now hungry and starts scrolling on Uber Eats.

Half an hour later, Glue texts Gwen again, reminds Gwen to not tell Mom and Dad and especially Lester that he interviewed at the school in Shenzhen. Glue also tells Gwen that even if he gets an offer from the school, he might prefer working for Lester full-time.

Gwen responds with a thumbs-up emoji. The emoji is yellow.

# SQUEEZE

# OUR

閂

# TONGUES

**GLUE IS** now an immigration consultant, a full-time employee at Lester Tse's firm. Glue scrolls through TikTok and Instagram. #fitnessaddict. Glue's TikTok algorithm is filled with workout videos. No more audiobooks. No more films. No more early 2000s Cantopop. All Glue does is work out with the tech bros who share the same floor as him. The building Lester Tse's office is in has a gym on the top floor equipped with a boxing ring. Glue stops playing basketball and takes up boxing. All the people he boxes with, after work, are tired and do not want to talk. Their communication is reduced to body movements in the ring. Glue does not know the names of his sparring partners. Glue gets Google alerts to keep himself up-to-date on cryptocurrency and the stock market. Gone are the days of reading Fanon. He does not read much at all lately. It is the beginning of December. Much has changed.

**WHEN GLUE** gets home, he watches YouTube and Reels on Instagram. He considers ordering McDonald's but having jerked off and stared at a screen for most of the day, Glue decides to put his phone away for a bit. Feeling hungry makes Glue recall how Elle, when they were waiting for food to arrive, would play a game called Cancel Me If You Can.

"So, do you come here often?" Elle asked Glue. They were waiting for their appetizers at a seafood restaurant near St. Lawrence Market. "Do you have oysters in China?"

"Um . . . Yes."

Elle wore an oversized fleece jacket and Levi's '90s jeans. "I heard that in China, they squat when they shit. So, I'm wondering, when you squat-shit, do you face the door of the stall or the wall?"

"Elle." Glue tried to keep his voice down. "What are you doing?"

"I just want to know, Mr. Wu. In case I have dirty oysters

in China and get diarrhea, which direction I should face. I might visit you one day, you know? If this night goes well, of course."

"I think I had oysters in China before and I was fine. Besides, we cook our oysters." Glue kept his tone serious.

"You Chinese like having all things cooked. Is that because of the government's overuse of pesticides? Why do you commies hate religion?" Elle paused, to look at Glue, who looked kind of stunned, before saying, loudly, "And women!"

"Elle!"

Everyone in the restaurant glanced over.

Elle started laughing.

All of a sudden, Glue remembers that he misses Elle. He also remembers, again, that he wants to die.

GLUE DOES not feel like eating anymore, just chugs two cartons of natural protein meal-replacement drinks he ordered from Taobao in bulk. He tries to shit but can't. He takes a shower while listening to a playlist on YouTube: "Korean rap music that provides me with the urge to pour milk in my bowl before cereal ☀ KHIPHOP PLAYLIST 한국 힙합 플레이리스트."[8]

Listening to music in languages Glue does not understand makes him feel safe. The hook of the first song goes like "We want our money back. We want our money back. We want our money back. We want our money back. We want our money back. Money back." Glue would recommend listening to this when taking a shower, not when taking a shit. Glue can't really explain why. When Glue gets out of the shower, he turns off his phone after setting an alarm, gets into bed with his hair still wet, and goes on his laptop. Tabs he has open: some Tencent Video, some government website with information about immigration, some Netflix K-drama he started watching at work when he was waiting for a client, and some YouTube video about easy-to-learn boxing moves that he opened but hasn't watched yet. Before he can watch the YouTube video, he has to watch a ten-second ad: a pair of thin lips are sucking soft rice noodles from a steaming bowl of soup. Glue can't focus on the video now that he has seen that ad. He cups his balls with his palm. His balls are not saggy. He started a new workout routine lately and is drinking more water. Glue is not sure if that helps his balls. It probably does. Glue will probably have to start eating tiger penis soup when he gets older. Or some other Chinese remedy to keep his dick going. Glue can't imagine not being able to masturbate. Glue forgets whom he learned this from, that a lot of white supremacists don't masturbate. This makes Glue want to masturbate even more. Glue wonders what would happen if he started eating tiger penis soup now. Glue's dick is getting hard. Glue sometimes wants to die. When he wants to die, he masturbates, which makes ejaculating feel better. Glue does not want to die now, though. Glue is starting to get hungry. Glue opens an incognito tab and goes on Pornhub. #interracial, #BDSM, #femdom, #whipping, #violent, #humanchair. An email notification pops on the top right corner of his screen, from OR Books—Glue must have subscribed to the platform when he was still in grad school. A book by a well-known philosopher. It is also a book about Mao. It uses this quote from Mao as the tagline: "天下大乱，形势大好" (Everything under heaven is in utter chaos; the situation is excellent). Glue deletes the email, unsubscribes, grabs some tissue, and goes back to his porn. The moment Glue comes, he feels like he needs to eat. The image of lips sucking rice noodles was waiting for him at the end of his orgasm; now he, too, wants to experience the sensation of having salty pork bone broth, warm, inside his mouth. The Tsui Wah Restaurant downstairs closes in an hour.

**18**

*GLUE IS* slurping his noodles. It is almost midnight. The Tsui Wah Restaurant will close soon. A skinny man with bleached blond hair eats his spaghetti with chopsticks. His other hand caresses the inner thigh of a Chinese woman next to him. Are they together? The woman looks annoyed. She's looking away, not responding to the man. She brushes the man's hand away from her lap, but he starts touching her back, and then her waist, and then her ass. He even slips his hand below her shirt and starts rubbing her back. A server walks over to their table to clear the empty dishes left behind by the previous customers. The man smirks at the server and places a used tissue on one of the empty plates. The server, a middle-aged Chinese woman with a bob cut and silver earrings, smiles politely at the man before reaching for the plate. The man pushes the plate a little further away from her, smirking all the while. The server is unfazed. She picks up another plate instead.

It's good that Glue is sitting near the entrance. From

here, he can see, from the window of this restaurant, on the pedestrian bridge that connects the Fu Tung Plaza and the Tung Chung MTR station, two police officers, one man and one woman, walking in his direction. Glue waits for a bit before calmly walking over to where the white man and the Chinese woman are sitting, keeping an eye on the police officers all the while. Glue needs to be certain that the two cops won't take too long to arrive at the scene.

Glue walks over to the two.

"You know this guy?" the man asks the woman. This man is speaking with spaghetti in his mouth and his hand under the woman's shirt.

Before the Chinese woman can respond, Glue kicks the stool the man is sitting on, knocking him off balance. Putting all his force into his arms, Glue grabs the man's hair and slams his face into the plate of spaghetti. Glue knees the man right in his liver—a move he learned from watching a YouTube video. Though Glue has never practised the move before, to his surprise, it works perfectly. The woman and the server scream. The man's chin hits the glass table and the table cracks.

Glue is holding the man's head down. The Chinese woman tries to push Glue away. It doesn't work. The man coughs, spits out some spaghetti. Blood is dripping from the table. The man tries to get up. Focusing all his force into his left leg, Glue knees the man in the stomach. The man gags, tomato sauce all over his face. Glue manages to knee the man in the stomach one more time before the

Chinese woman reaches for something to hit him with. A beer bottle would be best but Tsui Wah doesn't serve alcohol, so she hits Glue in the head with a dirty plate. Unlike in the movies, the plate doesn't break. Glue pushes the woman away and tries to knee the man one more time, but the two police officers run over.

"Woooo!" Glue screams and starts laughing to himself.

When the police officers tackle Glue, Glue does not resist. Glue thinks about dying, which makes him smile. The police officers look confused.

Having witnessed such a violent scene, the server is having trouble breathing. Medics are looking after her. She has on an oxygen mask. The Chinese woman who was with the man tells the police that she doesn't know the assailant, that he just walked over from the table across the restaurant and assaulted the two of them. Glue tells the cops that she's telling the truth.

Glue is arrested on the spot. As he is being escorted from the scene, he hears the people around him, the restaurant staff and the mall security guards, uttering the words "insane," "overworked," and "mentally ill."

The man Glue assaulted has his chin bandaged. His eyes are bruised. Glue is handcuffed. He has curry on his face, from the dirty plate the woman hit him with. The man gives Glue the middle finger as he walks by. Glue conjures up, in his mind, the smirk on the man's face when he was toying with the waitress. Glue smirks the same smirk back at the man.

In March 2021, a white man will attack an elderly Chinese woman in San Francisco. The Chinese woman will beat him up with a log and the man will be carried away on a stretcher. He will be bleeding, and his head will be bandaged. The man will give the woman the middle finger as he is being taken away by the medics. Glue will see this on an Instagram Reel. He will watch the video three times over. When he watches the video in the future, he will recall this moment in the present.

**ORIENTALISTS DO** not care for the rules and norms that locals have to abide by. Because of this, they are capable of violence. But Hong Kong, Glue learned from his primary school textbook, is a place for trade. To maintain the status of being the perfect place for commerce, stability is of the utmost importance. Hong Kongers must submit to keep things stable. Some Hongkies—especially those of an older generation—believe this wholeheartedly, albeit consciously or not: being indifferent to difference is how equality and, in turn, stability are achieved. Glue knows that he is no grassroots activist fighting for change. He will never be. He is no revolutionary. He will always be nothing more than an outsider, committing violent acts that disrupt the tranquility of this otherwise wonderful financial hub. Also, the only reason he knows how to use violence, he thinks, is because of his having been educated abroad, because of his own proximity to whiteness. What should Glue do? Glue starts singing the Chinese national anthem to himself:

*Arise, ye who refuse to be slaves!*
*With our flesh and blood, let us build a new Great Wall!*

Glue learned on Wikipedia that "March of the Volunteers" was a dramatic poem written by Tian Han, an activist fighting against the Japanese. But during the Cultural Revolution, the poet and playwright was imprisoned. After Tian's death, the song based on his poem was adopted for official use. Glue knows the song well—everyone here does. It plays before the evening news broadcast. But this is not the only reason why Glue remembers the lyrics to the song. *Let us build a new Great Wall.* Nothing ends. To "unite" and "strengthen" what we today refer to as China. The ones with power in China behave not unlike the white settlers of North America, whose violent crimes against Indigenous peoples are ongoing. China, in the name of modernization, is doing the same to the native populations in its autonomous regions. But now, Glue is beginning to think, and he never had such a thought before, that what China is doing is not too bad, that all of the shit China is doing to "catch up with America," the totalitarianism and neglect for human rights and environmental issues, things that Western media and China watchers criticize, are, on a practical level at least, not nearly as bad as genocide. The bar is low. This is made even more complicated: when China is criticized for its actions, it self-Orientalizes, reminds the rest of the world of its history of being colonized.

Memories of being a student in Hong Kong flash through Glue's mind. Once a year, Glue remembers, back when he was a student at the Queen's Music Academy in Diamond Hill, he watched, every school day before the July 1 holiday, the raising of the Hong Kong flag, the national flag of China, and the school flag which is purple with a gold outline of the Jehovahjireh Concert Hall, complete with its Christian cross on top, rising up to the polluted sky. Over a thousand students, in their summer uniforms—short-sleeve pastel-pink shirts with purple stripes and grey pants/skirts—watched from above, from outside their classrooms, as the marching band, marching in circles around the Roman battle arena, performed the tune of "March of the Volunteers." The funeral parlour across the street would be open. Smoke, on those days, would, as per usual, fill the air.

As Hong Kong comes closer to 2047, when the "one country, two systems"—and Hong Kong's days as a special administrative region—might end, many Hongkies are considering moving to the UK. "We are here because you were there" (Frantz Fanon, *The Wretched of the Earth*). *March on! March on! March, march on!*

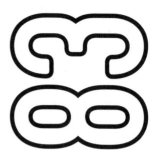

GLUE'S MANDARIN teacher, back when he was in high school, was an old Chinese man from a village in mainland China. Twice a semester, he would bring a radio to the classroom and play a recording of "March of the Volunteers." Why the radio? The classroom was equipped with an iMac and a built-in sound system. The entire class bullied this teacher, including Glue, saying that he was from a farm. Some called him a commie. Other students said he smelled of cows. Glue thinks of what Po-Wing told him, "I saw sixty-nine farmers laughing on the phone." Despite the bullying, the teacher continued to sing the national anthem alone. Some would mockingly sing along with him. No one listened to his lessons. No one in Glue's class, after three years, could speak Mandarin fluently.

Back when he was a teen, singing at karaoke bars on the weekends, Glue could get away with mumbling the words to sad Mandopop songs by Jay Chou because everyone was drunk and no one knew what Jay Chou, with his late 2000s mumble rap, was saying anyways. Now, handcuffed, Glue walks away from the scene he just caused. All the while, he is quietly singing the lyrics to "March of the Volunteers" to himself. But in Cantonese.

Glue is proud of himself. It is quite appropriate that this song is being voiced at this moment. Everything is forced. Glue's Cantonese pronunciation does not match the tone of the song, which makes him laugh. Glue continues singing. The notes to the song are low. Glue is out of tune, he knows. In his rendition of the song, all the revolutionary hot-bloodedness that the song provokes is completely removed. One of the police officers, hearing Glue, gives him a hostile look. Glue feels alienated. But, like his Mandarin teacher, Glue ignores that feeling and continues singing. Teenagers hanging out on the benches outside the mall are sipping bottles of Jolly Shandy and Smirnoff Ice as they film Glue on their smartphones.

"We can put a bag over your head if you want," says one of the officers. Glue must have lost his mask when he assaulted the couple.

Glue recalls the dream he had when he worked at Disneyland. The television host had to wear a black bag over her head.

Though Glue is shaking his head, he agrees to the bag and politely thanks the police officer.

Glue's head is held high, inside the bag. Glue marches forward.

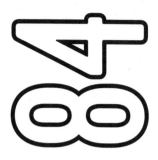

THE LOCAL news will probably cover this incident once. The footage the teenagers took might circulate online a few times, among Glue's Facebook friends. Perhaps there'll be a post about Glue on HKGolden: *This, it seems, is another case of a Kong dude's girl being taken by* 洋腸 (Western sausage). Netizens would probably look up Glue's background.

But none of this happens. There is a short thread, on Twitter, discussing why a former ESL instructor did such a thing to an innocent couple late at night. Other than that, Glue doubts anyone cares.

Glue does not care that no one cares.

When Glue was singing "March of the Volunteers" to himself, he was not thinking about the current Chinese Communist Party. He was singing the song, not for what it came to represent, but for what the words meant to him. He was thinking of Tian Han's poem. History marches on. *March on! March on! March, march on!*

*ELLE IS* smoking a cigarette on the balcony of the apartment that Glue and Gwen shared in Toronto. "I guess having sex with someone I had no feelings for was a way for me to gain a sense of balance."

When Elle told him this, Glue felt a cold chill creeping up his spine, making him want to vomit.

"In that moment, I just felt like I needed to have sex. So I did. It has nothing to do with you."

They were twenty-four then. Glue didn't say anything.

"I hope we can continue seeing each other, though."

"It's all right, Elle. I love you." Glue needed to say that. He needed his love to be reciprocated. He felt vulnerable. When he is vulnerable, he falls in love.

The two continued their relationship for a few more months. And then Elle left Glue to return to Singapore and Glue left Canada. Sitting in the police van and feeling the cold handcuffs on his wrists (which are sticky after the shift from the air-conditioned restaurant to the humidity of the outdoors), Glue remembers when he first landed in Hong Kong. As his Cathay Pacific flight descended from the sky, merging with the moisture of Lantau Island, he felt a sudden malaise, awakened to the fact that he had just left Canada to return here and perhaps might never go back. At certain moments, he still thinks about Elle. Glue just assaulted a man. Glue does not want to get back together with Elle anymore. Glue is a pervert. What he wants, at this moment, is to watch Elle have sex with another person. Perhaps Glue is finally coming to terms with his desires. If given the opportunity, Glue will not hesitate to drink Elle's urine, or let Elle step on his face. This, Glue now realizes, is what he truly wants. This is Glue's awakening. Glue thinks about Po-Wing, his old friend, his dealer. Glue imagines Po-Wing beating him. Glue imagines kissing Po-Wing. Watching Elle and that other person have sex, being beaten up by Po-Wing, is pleasure. All of this is what Glue, a twenty-six-year-old immigration consultant, wants right now. He wants to watch. He imagines himself watching himself watch the sex Elle is having with that other person through a hidden camera. Glue looks at himself through the rear-view mirror of the police van. Apart from the area around his eyes, his face is covered by a black bag. He focuses on his own eyes, his brown irises. He imagines himself watching himself watch Elle and that other person fuck.

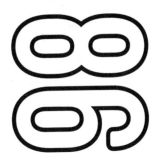

**GWEN GIVES** Glue a hug, drives him home, and tells him to rest.

"Are you sure you're good to go back to work next week?" Gwen asks.

Glue nods.

"Let's keep this away from Mom and Dad for now," Gwen says. "They're getting old. We should spare them. Also, the guy you fucked up, turns out he's here illegally— his visa expired. It doesn't seem like he'll be pressing any charges. If anything happens, Lester knows lawyers who can help you. You might have to do some mandatory community service or whatever here and there, and you won't be able to travel for some time, but everything should be okay for now."

Glue thinks about May and wonders what her real name might be. With so many people in such a small city, hiding the fact that you do not have a valid visa shouldn't be hard, especially if you're white. But out of everyone, Glue chose this guy to assault.

*Would you be happier if Mom and Dad were dead?* Glue doesn't ask Gwen this question. Perhaps the opposite is true. Glue and Gwen will feel even more guilty if their parents died. These thoughts are the precise opposite of familial piety, but Glue feels no guilt. His parents will be leaving Glue and Gwen their home in Macau, Glue's apartment (the mortgage for which still needs to be paid off), and the other properties they own in mainland China. Glue will probably sell all the properties and quit his job.

Glue remembers the night when he went out for a drive with May. That night, high on shrooms with May, Glue realized how self-righteous his father has always been. Making a point of not heckling and paying for things way above the market price is him allowing himself to continue benefiting from this system of inequality guilt-free. But Glue also remembers his parents' happy faces when Gwen, Lester Tse, and he were having lunch with them in Macau, the relief on his mother's face, looking at Glue's face. She thought Glue was slowly becoming financially stable.

"How old are Mom and Dad?" Glue asks Gwen.

"Dad's sixty-five. I think Mom's turning sixty."

"Do you think they're happy?"

"They don't care about that anymore, Glen Wu. Stop being such a romanticist. They just need to be at peace, knowing that the two of us can have secure lives." Gwen sighs. It looks as if it is about to rain. "I better get going. I'll see you later. Call me if you need anything."

Gwen treats Glue the same. It is as though Glue did not

just commit a violent act. This makes Glue a bit uncomfortable.

When Glue returns to his apartment, he realizes that the door to his sister's old room is open. The floor is clean, and the yellow-stained curtains have been replaced with clean cream-coloured blinds. There is a large, beautifully crafted rosewood desk and a silver floor lamp. A white light fixture is installed on the ceiling, and a sleek ergonomic office chair—the same model as those in Lester Tse's office—sits in the middle of the room. None of the furniture matches, but Glue knows that this is intentional. The old mattress on the floor is gone.

**LESTER TSE** is positive and energetic when Glue returns to work. It is as if nothing happened. No one at the office seems to notice that Glue was gone for an entire week. Or maybe everyone is doing an extremely good job at pretending they don't know. A colleague tells Glue that Michael Tam's ex called, asking for the details regarding Michael's plans to move to Calgary, saying that they have the right to know and that they are still Sandy's legal guardian. Putting on his most conservative, most professional face and tone, Glue tells the colleague that his client's information is confidential and that should they call again to ask about Mr. Tam's case, the firm will proceed to block their number and report them to the police.

After work, Glue receives a text from Lester Tse, telling him that he'll give him a ride home. "It'll be nice to have some company, you know? The traffic can get busy at this time. Plus, it might rain again later."

Lester Tse tells Glue that he is sorry for what happened. Sorry? Glue was, in every definition of the word, the assailant.

"Thanks for helping me out," Glue says to Lester Tse.

"Not necessary." Lester Tse genuinely sounds like he does not want to be thanked. "Can I ask you something, Glue?"

Lester Tse shuts the windows and turns on the air conditioner. All, all of a sudden, becomes quiet. Glue nods.

"Do you think Gwen is happy?"

"I don't think she's unhappy," Glue says honestly.

"I see."

Lester Tse drives a silver Lexus ES 300h. "I wouldn't be able to afford this at this age working in Canada," says Lester. "That's why I moved here. You and Gwen, you two are lucky. You have family here and all. My family's Chinese, but none of them, ever since they moved to Canada in the eighties, want to come back. They're perfectly content living in their house in Mississauga. They don't care about anything. They don't even vote. I've tried telling them to, many times—but none of them want anything to do with politics. All they care about is their own real estate business, making a stable income. Living there felt so isolating. I used to watch TVB. Those Kong-made TV shows, having loud family dinners, those used to make me so happy. I have to say, Glue. I very much enjoy being here, getting to have dim sum in Macau once in a while and being with your sister. I couldn't ask for anything better."

"We're happy to have you around." Glue feels he needs to say this. "Mom likes you a lot."

Lester Tse laughs. "They're nice people, your parents."

"How old are you?" Glue knows that Lester Tse is younger than Gwen, but how old he is exactly, Glue has no idea.

"Not much older than you," Lester Tse says. "I just turned twenty-seven." Two years younger than Gwen and a year older than Glue. Lester Tse is the middle child.

When Lester Tse arrives at Glue's apartment building, he tells Glue he has a gift for him, to welcome him back. In the brand-less paper bag are a bottle of brandy and three joints of pre-rolled weed. Lester Tse smiles and tells Glue to enjoy. Glue cannot tell if Lester Tse, by giving him this gift, is patronizing him or if he is being genuine. He must know that Glue dropped out of graduate school because he was in a drunken stupor, lost his student visa as a result, and had no choice but to return to Hong Kong.

"Want to smoke with me? Why don't you come up for a bit?" asks Glue.

"Next time. I've got to get to the airport to meet a client."

Glue thanks Lester Tse again and tells him that he will see him at the office tomorrow.

Glue's skin becomes moist the moment he leaves Lester's Lexus. The sky is still grey and the ground is wet and so is the air.

Drunk on Lester Tse's brandy, Glue texts May, asking if she wants to meet. May asks Glue if he is drunk. Glue lies and asks May if she wants him to accompany her to find her parents. She politely declines. Does May know that Glue, the week before, assaulted a man and was arrested? It doesn't matter. May would prefer to spend the night alone, she tells Glue, and suggests that they meet some other time, maybe Sunday evening. Some new private and public housing complexes have been built at the end of Man Tung Road. May asks if Glue would like to check them out with her then. "We can pick up beers at the 7-Eleven on the way."

It is nearing the end of December. It is no longer hot, no longer humid. The air is dry and damp. There was a clash between the protestors and the police the month before and a student died at the Hong Kong University of Science and Technology. The protests are beginning to die down as Covid regulations become stricter. Glue turns off his phone. All he wants right now is to have a drink with May.

# EVERY-

# THING

# SHRINKS

七

INTO A

#EUROTOUR

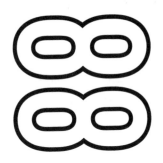

*ELLE TOLD* Glue that she loved him. Glue had never heard such words from anyone. Glue also did not know what to do with this information. Glue's parents never told him they loved him. Gwen never told Glue that she loved him either. But Elle did. Elle didn't seem nervous at all when she told Glue. "I love you," Elle said, simply. This happened the same night, on the rooftop, when the two were on edibles. They were laughing. It was cold. When Elle told Glue that she loved him, Glue's smile was genuine. "I love you too, Elle." When Glue said this, he felt both joy and guilt.

They broke up. The problem was not that Elle did not love Glue. He began to understand that, throughout the time they were together in Toronto, Elle was trying to justify her continued stay in Canada, away from her life in Singapore, where, because of her mother's fashion store and industry connections, she would be promised a successful career when she returned. Glue was supposed to be one of the reasons for Elle to stay. This is common. Hong

Kongers in Canada, in the US, England, and Australia stay with their romantic partners overseas, trying to become comfortable in a new country, trying to build a life away from home, to slowly become independent from their families, to assimilate in the country where they studied.

Towards the end of their relationship, a month or so before Glue left for Hong Kong and Elle left for Singapore, six months after Elle told Glue that she loved him and two weeks after Elle told Glue that she wouldn't want to live in Hong Kong, Elle had sex with someone else.

Context: Glue didn't want to see anyone else. Perhaps a part of Glue wanted to feel the pain of doing nothing while Elle saw other people. Now, Glue is beginning to understand why. Being Hong Kongese means dealing with the desire to find narratives to contextualize your sorrows. It is difficult to articulate the feeling of existing on borrowed time, between being a colony of a former empire and becoming a city in one of the largest countries in the world. In this polluted city, people gather outside MTR stations, trying to find their umbrellas that are at the bottom of their bags, perfectly folded into a slim silicone of fabric, unnoticeable beneath the laptops and files and wallets and bottled teas and makeup bags and sunscreen and glasses cases. Those whose bags do not contain an umbrella convene at the convenience stores located at the exits of MTR stations to purchase one only to feel guilty afterwards because in their small homes they have a pile of umbrellas, all of which have been used only once or twice. A fortunate few have partners and families who have the time and energy to care and come downstairs wearing their flip-flops, with umbrellas in their hands, to walk them home with their un-umbrellaed loved ones in the rain. At such moments, Glue would run home alone. He would be wet. He sometimes cried as he ran. He grew up in the 2000s. Cantopop singers back then, at least all the ones Glue listened to, were debuting their songs about heartbreak, and the Kong-made movies he watched were all about longing for a past loved one, a better time. They were about unrequited love. Even triad films bore such motifs. To be Hong Kongese is to feel trapped between cultures, political systems, and economic structures. It is to deal with a never-ending housing crisis. It is to want to leave but also to find a reason to not leave. It is to see all those around you leave, one immigration wave after another. It is to feel heartbroken, to miss a past where a better future was promised; it is to give your life to work without having a comfortable place to stay; it is to be on the receiving end of different forms of state violence. It is to run home alone in the rain without an umbrella, crying and enjoying it. All of this, Glue grew up thinking, was romantic. As a result, he decided to remain heartbroken. Elle was not to blame. No one was. Elle seeing other people, and Glue not doing anything about it, was what Glue was bound to do in that situation. This is perfect. Context is everything. Glue was finally able to have a story to contextualize all he felt and grew up feeling.

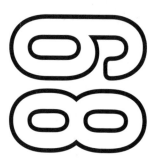

THE HONG Kong dollar is pegged to the American dollar, which stabilizes the currency but contributes to artificially low interest rates, which, in turn, contributes to the high property prices. Glue understands that everything is about maintaining stability. This is one of the many reasons why Hong Kong is the most unaffordable place on the planet. But the housing crisis started long before the peg in 1983. In the 1940s, only colonizers were allowed to live on the Peak, overlooking Hong Kong Island, now the most expensive place to live on earth, with tacky-ass apartments costing up to HK$509.6 million (CAN$81 million). We've made progress, though. Now, it's not just the colonists (the Brits seem to prefer the word "expatriate"); anyone in the 1 percent can live there as well. (You are rich because you are white, you are white because you are rich.) The rich keep fucking each other and selling and reselling property to each other. Glue remembers reading in a *South China Morning Post* article that the monthly income of the top 10 percent is over forty-four times that of the bottom ten. This divide continues to grow. To maintain the order of this financial hub, everything needs to be controlled. Because stability is always the priority. Nothing can change. The poor need to remain poor, the government believes, because the poor won't work (continue to suffer for the rich) if they are given money. Since most of the land here is owned by the government, the state can keep taxes low and investments coming in. This has been successful. Evidence of the policy's success is that over a million of Hong Kong's 7.4 million people live below the poverty line. This number doesn't really go down.

May is in her usual attire. Gym shorts. Her white Nike windbreaker is zipped all the way up. Glue shouldn't have worn a tank top. Mosquitoes continue to harass his arms as they walk through the Tung Chung North Park. They pass by the primary school that Glue attended for a few years before transferring to the Queen's Music Academy. A large light blue banner hangs on the gate of the school, listing the names of ten students who were accepted to reputable universities. One of the three hundred students graduating will be attending the University of Hong Kong in the fall. The student's name is on the very top of the banner. Glue doesn't tell May that he used to attend this school.

Streetlights light up the road. None of the apartments above them have their lights on.

"They're going to be filled with people starting next week," May says. "If you're lucky, you get an apartment with a view of the sea and the airport."

The two look up at the thousands of empty apartments. It feels as if this part of the world has just ended. It is finally peaceful. The apartments on the left, at this private estate, the Visionary, each have large windows and a balcony. There is also a gate at the entrance and a sign, in Chinese and English, noting that only authorized personnel are allowed to enter. The twelve buildings, each around fifty storeys high, form an L shape. In between the buildings is a pool; a clubhouse that is equipped with a theatre; a gym; a tennis court; a playground; a yoga studio; and a café. There is also a tropical garden on top of the parking lot. There are palm trees everywhere, too. Just across the street, however, is a cluster of grey buildings with small windows. Perhaps to add some flair to the concrete exteriors, there are green, orange, and yellow stripes painted straight down from the tops of these buildings, to colour-code the pile of concrete structures. This is the Ying Tung Estate. It has no gate. Next to it is a mall, where restaurants, a wet market, a supermarket, convenience stores, a library, and pharmacies will be located. To get to live here, you need luck. If your household income is below a certain threshold, you can enter a draw. Some will get to buy a unit.

"Weed?" Glue asks.

May nods. Glue takes out the pre-rolls that Lester Tse gave him, which taste way smoother than the watery stuff Po-Wing has. For a moment, Glue is annoyed by how good this weed tastes, so sweet and calming. Glue laughs after taking a few puffs.

May says, "I heard they're going to try to build two artificial islands off of Lantau Island in a few years. The project's called Lantau Tomorrow Vision. Have you heard of it? I hate the name, but I want to be here when it's done. Imagine an entire island, in Hong Kong, filled with empty buildings and no people. That's amazing, isn't it?"

"Do you know when you'll be leaving yet?" Glue has no interest in Lantau Tomorrow Vision, which, in any case, is no name for an island.

May just continues walking.

"I was arrested," Glue says.

"I saw. That was hilarious."

"Hilarious?"

"Turns out the guy can't press any charges. You must have thought you'd stir up such a shitstorm."

Glue doesn't know what to say. But soon he starts laughing with May.

They sit on the bench of one of the bus stops. No buses are scheduled to work the routes of this part of the island until next month. They can see the airport. No planes. They can also see the first of three artificial islands that connect the undersea tunnel that connects to the Hong Kong–Zhuhai–Macao Bridge. The elementary school behind them is empty. A bulldozer leaves a construction site. This Sunday evening is quiet.

"Let's go," May says. She grabs Glue by the arm, where mosquito bites are forming red bumps on the top of his skin.

**7-ELEVEN PLASTIC** bags in hand, they continue walking through this empty section of Lantau Island, strolling aimlessly through the unpopulated land in the most unaffordable place on earth. Glue holds on to May's elbow as they walk, which, though it's warm right now, feels cold.

"Was there a five-hundred-dollar bill in your jacket?" Glue asks.

"No," says May.

May gives Glue a cookie. It tastes quite good for an edible.

"Are you high?" Glue asks.

"I will be soon." May finishes the rest of the cookie. "Happiness is like cookies your brain bakes for itself," she announces. "A cognitive scientist said that happiness, like a cookie, is merely a tool. When you are young, you always want to eat cookies. But once you get older, you realize that eating cookies is just an instrument to make you go back to eating vegetables. Eventually, you stop eating sweets altogether because you don't want diabetes."

"Are you happy right now?" Glue can't help but ask.

"I don't know," says May. "Glue, who was the 'you' in 'Deeping Yellows'?"

Glue pauses, wondering what it would mean for him to answer May's question, to break the rules of their relationship. Would it change their relationship? Would they begin to be honest with each other? Would they fall in love? Probably not. Yet falling in love is always a possibility.

This thought makes Glue feel vulnerable. It is Glue's turn to feel as though a shrimp is swimming inside him. Glue always enjoys being with May. In the empty streets of Lantau Island, where all the mountains that surround them are becoming one with the night and the MTR is no longer running and the yellow lights from the airport are flickering but no planes are landing, Glue looks at May. The skin of her face, a little bit oily, glitters under the streetlight; the word "comrade" comes to Glue's mind.

"Her name is Elle. We lived in Toronto together," Glue says, breaking the rules, rendering all the time they spent following the rules meaningless. "Then we broke up. She went back to Singapore and I came back here. I've actually walked through this neighbourhood with her. Back then, none of this was built, of course. The summer after we got together, she visited me in Hong Kong and we went to the Indian restaurant, the Seaview Café, at the pier near here. Have you been?"

May shakes her head. There is a moment of silence before May asks, "Were the two of you happy together?"

"Sometimes."

"Sometimes." May repeats the word to herself quietly. "Whenever I feel happy," May says, "I also always feel kind of guilty."

Glue murmurs to show he understands. May too, it seems, is also ready to break the rules. May is a comrade.

"In England, after I graduated, I spent an extra month in Sussex. I didn't do jackshit, didn't look for work, didn't study, just spent my parents' money with this boy I met, another international student from Hong Kong. I felt no hurry to find work. It was a time for a break. I was supposed to be happy. And I was. I didn't have to wake up early for class. I exercised when I wanted. I started smoking when I was eighteen, but for a while, didn't even feel the need to smoke cigarettes. But after two weeks or so." May pauses. "Yeah, two weeks or so later, I started feeling guilty for being happy."

Glue needs a moment to find his words. He's a bit drowsy and dehydrated from only drinking alcohol for the entire evening. "Now that you're looking back," Glue says, "do you know why you felt sad?"

"I'm just like that, I guess. I can never indulge in anything completely. I have a feeling that you feel the same way as well, Glue."

Glue is reminded of the time he worked at Disneyland. Families and their children were escaping their realities in Hong Kong, spending money and time to travel to a place where reality is suspended.

"I didn't know how to be happy with my boyfriend either," May says. "Every day we would walk around the town. We would cook together, go for runs, and drink a bit of wine at night. Everything was how I imagined retirement would look like."

Permanent Vacation—that's a good movie title. It's a good title, Glue thinks, because "Vacation" is a strange word. Vacation in Chinese is 度假 (dou⁶ gaa in Cantonese or, in Mandarin, dùjià). 假, if pronounced ga² or jiǎ, means "fake." When we're on vacation we are always faking. Glue remembers when he was younger, when he and Gwen and his parents were on vacation, when they walked along the beaches in Phuket, he felt fake, felt the four of them were performing a middle-class family in Hong Kong going on vacation to Thailand. He felt uncomfortable then, was a grumpy fifteen-year-old for the entire trip. He felt like he was forcing himself to swim, to stroll the night markets, to spend time away from Hong Kong with his family—a secular Hongkie family's idea of a Christmas holiday. "What do you want?" Gwen had asked. "You're so upset the whole trip. What's wrong?"

Glue didn't know what to say. At the resort, facing the beach, when he thought his sister was asleep, he cried into his pillow, which was fluffy and clean and smelled like nothing.

Glue looks at May, who is looking at the road, lit by yellow streetlights. May probably notices that Glue is looking at her but she doesn't look back. She takes another sip of beer.

Glue, when he takes his eyes off May, comes to a realization, based on a feeling: May will be leaving Hong Kong soon. She will return to England. Glue, for a second, considers asking May to confirm his speculation. It is such a simple question to ask. "May, will you be leaving soon?" But Glue doesn't ask May this again.

May breaks the silence. "Do you miss her, Glue? Do you miss Elle?"

"Not anymore," Glue says, almost instinctively. This surprises even Glue himself. Is it true that Glue no longer misses Elle? Glue notices that, since he decided to become an ESL instructor, he had stopped trying to call Elle. He stopped stalking her social media accounts as well. Glue has realized something about himself: he has the tendency to make himself feel more trapped than he actually is. This is why he did not become a writer. When he tried to become a writer, back in Toronto, back when he felt inspired by Elle, when the two spent weekends devouring films, this was when he gave Elle hope. This, perhaps, made Elle feel free as well.

**THEY ARE** back at May's apartment. May wraps a tie across Glue's eyes and ties a tight knot. "Do me a favour, Wu Ga-Ling."

Coming from May, Glue's Chinese name feels foreign. No one, in a long time, has addressed Glue with his Chinese name, not even Glue's parents. Glue was Glen Wu was Glue. Not Wu Ga-Ling.

"Imagine that I'm pointing a gun at you."

"What?"

"And stop speaking English. Speak Cantonese from now on," she says. "And remember, there's a gun being pointed at your right temple."

"知道," Glue says, accepting his identity as Wu Ga-Ling, and by doing so, accepting the reality that Wu Ga-Ling inhabits, one where a gun is pointed at his head, and only Cantonese is spoken.

"Our minds are nothing more than simulators and experiencers," May says. May grabs Wu Ga-Ling's hair and puts his head between her legs. Wu Ga-Ling hears a click. Does May actually have a gun? She presses Wu Ga-Ling's head down and brings her legs closer together. Wu Ga-Ling starts moving his tongue inside her. She pulls his hair harder. Wu Ga-Ling raises his head. May slaps him in the face and pushes his head down once more, holding him tight between her legs. This time, Wu Ga-Ling indulges in May's wetness, his tongue's movements becoming slower and more precise. The feeling of cold metal pressing against Wu Ga-Ling's temple seems to be emerging from within him, somewhere beneath his skull. *Our minds are nothing more than simulators and experiencers*—May's words echo in Wu Ga-Ling's mind. Wu Ga-Ling continues licking and the feeling of the gun being pressed against his temple becomes more and more real.

May says something in English, but what? In this reality, all of Wu Ga-Ling's thoughts are confined within a single language, Cantonese.

Glue ejaculates.

The next morning, Glue is not hungover—quite the opposite. Everything seems further away, and clearer. Glue's feet touch the floor. Although Glue is performing the familiar motions of standing up, his movements feel far away, as if his mind, or rather, his consciousness, has become disinterested in his bodily existence. His consciousness is slowly retreating and becoming a mere observer of this skinny Chinese body of his.

Glue gently shuts the door to the bedroom, where May

is still asleep, and opens the blinds in the living room. Planes take off—like secrets no one remembers ever existed, they disappear silently into the polluted sky. Glue sees a durian on May's dining table. He places the tip of his index finger on one of the durian's spikes. He presses into it. He bleeds.

Glue should go home and take a shower. Before he leaves the apartment, he steals the copy of *Employees F1rst: Inspire, Engage, and Focus on the HEART of Your Organization* and tosses it in the recycling bin downstairs.

*GLUE IS* back home. Warm water from the shower lands on the back of Glue's neck and runs down his spine. Glue comes to a realization (based on a feeling): his identity is not fixed. He might have known this all along, but now, he is more aware of the fact that his memories, on which his identity is based, are something intangible. His identity feels stable only because of the illusion of continuity.

Glue would much rather be a machine than an immigration consultant. If someone were ever to offer to upload Glue's consciousness to a machine, Glue would choose to be a Roomba. His purpose would be clear: to clean.

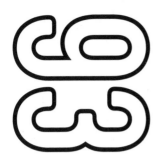

*GLUE IS* lying on his bed, naked. It is night. His windows are open. His air conditioner is turned off. Glue is remembering what he did before his violent act. When Glue assaulted the man, he was drunk. He'd watched forty-five minutes' worth of hardcore pornography before heading downstairs to eat—#interracial, #BDSM, #femdom, #whipping, #violent, #humanchair.

It was raining. Glue was in bed. His laptop was pressed against his chest. The bottle of whiskey was beside him. On the corner of his screen was an ad, suggesting that he subscribe to a film channel. Ads for art-house film channels popped up constantly, because Glue is still Facebook friends with people he met in theatre school, people who use such platforms.

The film channel was screening a series by Yasujirō Ozu. Glue, at one point, wanted to start exploring Ozu's works with Elle, but had trouble accessing the translated versions of the films. This would be the perfect moment for Glue to rediscover his interest. If Glue clicks the ad and sub-scribes to this film channel, there's a chance he will recon-nect with his love of stories, which might lead to him writing something. It wouldn't matter that it is too late for Glue to submit to his former professor's ecology project.

He didn't do this, of course. He unsubscribed to such channels. He also felt as though he would never again have the patience to watch slow films. He tried to masturbate himself to sleep. It didn't work. He became hungry because he watched a commercial for Taiwanese rice noodles. Unable to sleep, Glue, around midnight, decided to head downstairs to eat. He assaulted a man. He got arrested.

But let's say, if all of that didn't happen, if Glue did end up staying at home and watching a film by Ozu, would he have written something?

We can only speculate. So, let's do just that.

Using what we know about Glue, let's complete the writing assignment for him. Word limit: 150.

## Language Learners

Every motion is a gesture. You say this about rain in films by Ozu. A gesture's meaning comes from the response it elicits. When you respond to a gesture, the meaning of your response is sent simultaneously to the preceding gesture and the gestures that come after. Everything we do is in dialogue with something else, but sometimes AI systems struggle to understand this outside a game of Go, where not all the rules are set. So I resort to asking my students to close their eyes. Listen to the sounds around you, I say, think of all noises as gestures and respond to them with gestures of your own. But they don't move. One breath after another, the classroom's breathing becomes heavier and heavier; each breath, now a response to the one that came before, gives meaning to the ones that come after.     An organism is formed.

(150 words)

*About the author*

Glen Ga-Ling Wu (he/him, born 1993) is a writer and educator born in Hong Kong.

Glue will never write this. It continued to rain in Tung Chung, and whenever it rains, Glue feels as though he should drink more. Glue took a sip of whiskey, got back into bed, and watched an ad for Taiwanese rice noodles and a YouTube video, before returning to Pornhub.

*"DO YOU* like it back here, in Hong Kong?" If Elle and Glue meet, this is probably one of the first questions Elle will ask.

"I don't know." This will probably be Glue's honest answer. "But I don't miss Toronto's cold, scentless winters."

Elle, in the summer of 2017, visited Glue in Hong Kong. They visited a joint little known about, Seaview Café at the Tung Chung Pier. Only fishermen use that pier and the café, which serves Indian food and opens only for lunch. The place is small. There is no air conditioning, only blue ceiling fans. There, Glue and Elle played a game.

"Let's play a game!" Elle suggested. "It's called Inconsistent Lists. So, let's say, if the topic is film, then we have to write a list of favourite films that are entirely unrelated. Imagine that someone with no personality whatsoever is creating this list." Glue and Elle started writing lists on a napkin.

Inconsistent list of top five films:

> 1) *Sex and the City 2*, 2010
> 2) *Human Flow*, 2017
> 3) *The Birth of a Nation*, 1915

"No!" Elle said. "*The Birth of a Nation* is too much of the opposite of *Human Flow*. It's too binary, not random at all. It needs to be more complex."

"What about *The Human Centipede*?"

> 3) ~~*The Birth of a Nation, 1915*~~ *The Human Centipede*, 2009
> 4) *Ponyo*, 2008
> 5) National Geographic

"Let's try musicians."

> 1) LL Cool J
> 2) Yo-Yo Ma
> 3) Nina Simone
> 4) Limp Bizkit
> 5) G-Dragon

A little tipsy from the bottle of pinot noir they finished, they continued discussing consistently inconsistent lists as they walked back to Glue's.

Inconsistent list of top five favourite actors:

1) Ronald Reagan
2) Tobey Maguire
3) Lupita Nyong'o
4) Bruce Lee
5) Kourtney Kardashian

Inconsistent list of top five favourite fashion brands:

1) FILA
2) Kirkland Signature (by Costco)
3) Dior
4) Hollister
5) NASA (by NASA Depot, apparel for space lovers)

That was two years ago. 2019 is coming to an end soon. Glue is having a coffee at the Starbucks near Tung Chung Bus Terminal. It is eight in the morning. The cabin attendants who are gathering outside the terminal look too perfect— the N95 masks they have on cause their delicate eye makeup and beautifully coiffed hair to stand out more. Hong Kong's humidity does not seem to affect their looks one bit. It's as though they don't belong to the same reality. A crew from Emirates, dressed in their perfectly straight mushroom-coloured suits and maroon hats, are waiting for the rest of their crew to arrive before boarding their bus.

Glue is in shorts and a windbreaker. None of the elegantly dressed attendants even glance in Glue's direction. Cabin attendant, as an occupation, especially with the impending pandemic, will probably be automated away soon. Glue, though a ten-minute walk from his apartment, feels as if he's in a zoo, looking at endangered animals. But then again, who is Glue to think that? Aren't some of the jobs he is "qualified" to do also endangered? With so many language apps and so much new software being developed, will we still need ESL teachers? If so, working as an immigration consultant might be the most meaningful thing he has going on.

The pilots always arrive last. A crew from Cathay Pacific assembles in the lobby before boarding their bus, and a team from Etihad Airways follows.

Staring at the cabin crews, Glue gets a text. It is May. She has decided to return to England. *I always had a feeling that you knew I would be leaving soon. Still, I'm sorry I didn't tell you earlier. I don't know if you've ever felt the same way, but the time we spent together was very important to me. It makes leaving a little harder.* May also says that she will be in touch when she arrives in London.

Glue will leave May on read before responding. Glue is not mad, though. He's glad that she is able to leave and return freely. But a pandemic is coming and travelling will become increasingly difficult. Glue doesn't know this at the time, but May will not return to Hong Kong until four years later, in 2023, after the Hong Kong government finally lifts the mandatory hotel quarantine. Glue also recalls, as he sips his generic Starbucks coffee this hazy Sunday morning, waiting for his phone to connect to the coffee shop's Wi-Fi, on this patio stuck between Pret A Manger's patio and Shake Shack's (which does not open until eleven), that last night he was on the toilet, on his phone, constipated once more, scrolling through Instagram Reels. He sees a clip. The clip is from a podcast. It is May, in her usual athleisure wear. She has her hair tied up and she seems to be in her Tung Chung apartment, interviewing a person in a King Kong costume in her living room. May is asking the King Kong, in an almost accusatory tone, a series of questions. "Who the hell are you? What made you think you could show up like this? Who are you?" May repeats, her tone stern, "Why aren't you answering my questions?"

The King Kong puts his palms on his head, ready to take off his mask.

"Don't you dare take that off."

King Kong lowers his arms. The clip ends.

When his phone is finally connected to the Starbucks Wi-Fi, Glue tries to find the clip. It might have been real. He hasn't been sleeping too well and sometimes finds himself awake in the middle of the night, sitting on the toilet, scrolling through his phone. But this morning, he finds that he is unable to log in to his Instagram account. *The password you entered was incorrect.* After a few attempts, Glue gives up. Instead of attempting to reset his password, Glue deletes the app.

Continuous existence is an illusion in the first place. At the core, we're all completely empty. The tool, Glue realizes, that binds the "Glue" from this coffee shop and the

"Glue" from the day he wrote the lists with Elle is the thought/illusion/belief that the present Glue has memories of the Glue who wrote the lists (and of Elle, of course). This sense of continuity between events is, to borrow May's expression, much like happiness, a cookie, nothing more than a tool that allows Glue to convince himself that he is himself. Glue is a machine that thinks that he is Glue, nothing more. When Glue's body stops functioning, someone can upload all his memories (data) to another machine (a Roomba) that thinks that it is Glue (continuity).

This realization makes Glue feel all right that May has left. Glue hopes that May is happy, whether she is back in England or in Hong Kong hosting an absurdist podcast featuring a man dressed as King Kong.

It is Christmas. Plastic lights are tied around trunks of the palm trees planted outside the Tung Chung MTR station. It is cold. It just rained. There are puddles everywhere. People are lining up outside restaurants, waiting to be seated for morning tea and dim sum. It is still raining a little, but the sun is out. A young couple, holding Starbucks coffees and an umbrella, passes by with their dog. A group of seniors are practising tai chi in the pagoda.

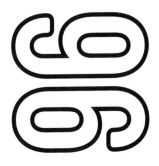

*GLUE DOES* not leave Hong Kong. He will stay in Hong Kong throughout the pandemic. Glue will watch as the Beijing security law passes. Glue will try, again, to work in mainland China at some point in the future. Glue will work there for a bit and inevitably return to Hong Kong. Glue will not meet May when she returns to Hong Kong in 2023 because Glue will have Covid. The two will meet in England, once, in December of 2024 and Glue will tell May that he felt that he could have fallen in love with her when the two were driving around in the New Territories and May will tell him that she had feelings for him too and felt as though she could have fallen in love with him when she saw him sitting on the staircase, beers between his thighs, outside the 7-Eleven that night. In 2024, Glue will also find out what May's real name is. They will laugh and Glue will tell May that he is glad that the two met back then. Glue will travel around Europe, alone, for two weeks. He will cry when walking around alone in Rome before returning to Hong Kong, back to his Tung Chung apartment. Glue will have dinner with Lester Tse and Gwen, just the three of them. The three of them will hang out more after Gwen and Lester get married. Glue will learn to enjoy their company. Glue will continue to stay here, in Tung Chung, in Hong Kong, working for Lester Tse but he will also teach English again on the weekends, something he hated doing back when he was in Toronto. He will not visit Toronto until he is in his mid-thirties. Travelling that far will always be too expensive. But all of this will happen in the future.

**NOW**, it is still 2019. Glue is alone, in Starbucks. May just told him she left. Glue isn't too far away from the restaurant near the pier he went to with Elle. Glue stopped visiting the joint some years ago. He remembers sharing vermicelli kheer with coconut milk there with Elle. The restaurant was not equipped with air conditioning, only blue ceiling fans. There weren't any lights, either. The dining area was lit completely by the small electric candles on each table that were probably from Ikea. Glue has the same candles at home. Occasionally, fishermen arrived at the pier. Elle and Glue watched from the window as the fishermen docked, the waves nudging their little blue fishing boats gently against the shoreline rocks. It's barely lunchtime. Glue starts walking towards the pier. He is not certain that the place will even be open.

## ACKNOWLEDGEMENTS

A huge thank you to my incredible editor, Deborah Sun de la Cruz. I could not ask for a better, more inspiring editor to work with. Thank you for bringing out the best in the writing that makes up *Batshit Seven*.

Thank you to my agent, Kelvin Kong, for your care and support. I would also like to thank the copyeditor, Shaun Oakey, and the designer, Matthew Flute. Thank you both for engaging with *Batshit Seven* in such a meaningful and inspiring way.

Thank you to everyone who has given me feedback on this project: Ashish Seth, Simone Dalton, Greg Rhyno, and John Currie from The North Writers Group. Thank you to the South Asian Visual Arts Centre and all the artists who were part of the 2020–2021 Ada Dada Residency: CAM Collective (Carisa Antariksa, Amreen Ashraf, Maria Denise Yala), Saira Chhibber, Vishal Kumaraswamy, Lingxiang Wu, and a special thank you to Maria Alejandrina Coates, for your incredible organizational skills and generosity. Finally, I need to thank the digital artist Maari Sugawara for being the first to discuss my ideas with me throughout the writing of *Batshit Seven*.

I began this project in Toronto. It was the winter of 2019, right before the Covid pandemic. From 2019–2023, I worked on *Batshit Seven* while traveling between Canada and China. I would like to extend my thanks to all those who were with me and supported me throughout the travels, lockdowns, and quarantines: Kevin Jae, Chen Zhong, Selin Kepenek, Luyao, Zahid Daudjee, Jade Shi, Jeremy Hao, Edward Zhang, Louie Yilong Liu, Maari Sugawara, EJ Anupol, Nawang Tsomo, Guanjiao Long, Baldwin Yuen, Prisca Tang, Siti Rohani, and Mom and Dad.

SHEUNG-KING is the pen name of Aaron Tang. He was born in Vancouver and grew up in Hong Kong. His debut novel, *You Are Eating an Orange. You Are Naked.*, was a finalist for the 2021 Governor General's Award, a finalist for the 2021 Amazon Canada First Novel Award, longlisted for CBC's Canada Reads 2021, and named one of the best book debuts of 2020 by *The Globe and Mail*. He taught creative writing at the University of Guelph, where he received his MFA in creative writing. He now divides his time between Canada and China. *Batshit Seven* is his second novel.

"Surprising, bizarre, and
perhaps most of all, fun."
NABEN RUTHNUM, AUTHOR OF *A HERO OF OUR TIME*

"Like a glass-bottom boat tour
of the millennial mind."
MICHAEL LAPOINTE, AUTHOR OF *THE CREEP*

"Elegantly styled and full
of raucous humour."
ADNAN KHAN, AUTHOR OF *THERE HAS TO BE A KNIFE*

"Another masterpiece of fiction
from one of the freshest voices in
Asian Canadian lit today."
JENNY HEIJUN WILLS, AUTHOR OF
*OLDER SISTER. NOT NECESSARILY RELATED.*